POISON AND POTIONS

A SPELLBOUND BOOKSHOP PARANORMAL COZY MYSTERY

BOOK 4

J. A. WHITING

Copyright 2024 J.A. Whiting and Whitemark Publishing

Cover copyright 2024 Signifer Book Design

Formatting by Signifer Book Design

Proofreading by Donna Rich (donnarich@me.com) and Riann Kohrs (www.riannkohrs.com)

This book is a work of fiction. Names, characters, places, or incidents are products of the author's imagination or are used fictitiously. Any resemblance to locales, actual events, or persons, living or dead, is entirely coincidental.

All rights reserved.

No part of this publication can be reproduced or transmitted in any form or by any means, electronic or mechanical, without permission in writing from J. A. Whiting.

To hear about new books and book sales, please sign up for my mailing list at:
jawhiting.com

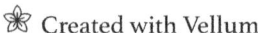 Created with Vellum

Use your magic for good

1

As the morning sun peeked through the window, the alarm gently roused Shelby Price from her peaceful slumber. She stretched lazily, her long, wavy brown hair splayed across the soft pillows of her comfortable bed. Shelby's brown eyes fluttered open, taking in the familiar surroundings of her bedroom in the apartment located above her beloved bookshop, Spellbound Books.

With a contented sigh, the young woman rose from bed and began her daily morning routine. She padded softly into the kitchen, where she was greeted by the gentle purring of her loyal companion and familiar, Harper. The majestic part Maine Coon cat, with her long, silky fur of gray, white, and black, twined affectionately around Shelby's legs as she prepared the cat's breakfast.

"Good morning, sweet girl," Shelby cooed, running her fingers over Harper's soft fur. "Ready for another day at the shop?"

"I sure am," Harper said to Shelby's mind. The cat's green eyes shone with intelligence and understanding. Even before Shelby developed the ability to hear her cat speaking to her, she'd always felt a special connection with her feline friend.

As the young woman sipped her morning tea, she gazed out the window, admiring the picturesque view of Hamlet, Massachusetts. The charming seaside village, known for its rich history and quirky residents, held a special place in Shelby's heart. Growing up in Hamlet, surrounded by her close-knit family—her parents, John and Ginny, her brother, Adam, and her grandparents, Tom and Mary—she'd always dreamed of owning her own bookshop, and now, that dream was a reality.

For a few moments, Shelby's thoughts drifted to her childhood and memories of lazy summer days spent exploring the rocky coastline with friends and pleasant evenings curled up with a good book by the fireplace. Her parents had instilled in her a deep love for literature, and her grandparents had regaled her with tales of Hamlet's fascinating history, including the legend of the mysterious Harris family and their rumored treasure.

"Come on, Harper. Let's get to work."

With a smile on her face, Shelby descended the stairs to Spellbound Books, ready to start another day. With the cat beside her, she unlocked the door and stepped inside, inhaling the comforting scent of books and the faint aroma of vanilla candles lit the previous day. Shelby had worked to create a warm and inviting atmosphere in her shop, with reading nooks, overstuffed armchairs, and well-stocked shelves brimming with literary treasures.

Just after she flipped the sign on the door to "Open," she heard the cheerful jingling of the bell above the entrance. Rachel, her part-time employee and good friend, walked in, her long, dark curls bouncing with each step and a bright smile on her face.

"Morning, Shelby," Rachel greeted, her bubbly personality already filling the shop with positive energy. "You'll never guess what happened last night."

Shelby grinned, knowing that Rachel was always eager to share the latest gossip in town. "Tell me. What's got you so excited this early in the morning?"

Rachel leaned against the counter, her eyes sparkling with excitement. "Well, you know how I've been crushing on Chad, the cute barista from Bread and Roses? He wants us to be exclusive. We're only going to date each other. Can you believe it?"

Shelby clapped her hands together, genuinely happy for her friend. "That's wonderful. I'm so thrilled for you. You two make such an adorable couple."

"I'm so nervous, though," Rachel confessed, twirling a strand of her hair around her finger. "I really like him, and I want this to be perfect."

Shelby placed a reassuring hand on Rachel's shoulder. "Just be yourself. Chad is lucky to have someone as kind and caring as you."

The two friends continued to chat, brainstorming ideas for a new window display in the bookshop. Their easy banter and laughter filled the store, creating a warm and welcoming atmosphere for the customers who began to arrive.

As the morning progressed, Shelby greeted each patron with a smile and a helpful attitude. She assisted a young boy in finding the perfect adventure book, recommended a thought-provoking novel to a college student, and helped an elderly lady locate a classic romance she had been searching for.

Her love for books and vast knowledge of the town's history shone through in her interactions with customers. She shared stories of Hamlet's past, such as the tale of the brave fishermen who rescued a shipwrecked crew during a terrible storm and the legend of the ghostly figure said to haunt the old lighthouse on the cliffs.

During a lull in business, Shelby took a moment to appreciate the charm of her shop. She let her eyes run over the spines of the books, marveling at the wealth of stories and knowledge contained within their pages. In an age of online retailers, running an independent bookstore was no easy feat, but for Shelby, promoting the joys of reading and connecting with her customers face-to-face made every challenge worthwhile.

As the day drew to a close, she and Rachel began tidying up the shelves and display tables. They chatted about their plans for the evening, with Rachel gushing about her upcoming date with Chad and Shelby sharing her excitement for her weekly drum circle session with her best friend, Lucy.

"Have fun with Chad tonight," Shelby said, a mischievous glint in her eye. "You'll have to tell me all about it tomorrow."

Rachel blushed, her cheeks turning a soft shade

of pink. "I promise I will. Now I need to hurry home and get ready."

With a quick hug, Rachel dashed out of the shop, leaving Shelby to finish the closing tasks. As she was about to lock up, Harper meowed just before the bell above the door chimed once more, signaling the arrival of Shelby's best friend, Lucy Blake.

Lucy, a talented pastry chef with chin-length blonde hair and sparkling blue eyes, greeted Shelby with a warm embrace. "Ready for our weekly dose of drumming?"

Shelby nodded enthusiastically. "Absolutely, but first, let's head up to my apartment for dinner. I've got a delicious slow-cooker chili waiting for us."

The two friends made their way up the stairs with Harper leading the way, the aroma of the hearty chili wafting through the air. In Shelby's apartment, they sat down to a comforting meal of chili, fresh salad, and warm garlic bread.

"So, how are things going at the B and B?" Shelby asked, taking a sip of her iced tea.

Lucy's face lit up with excitement. "You know how I've been experimenting with some new pastry recipes? Well, the guests have been raving about them. The owner even mentioned the possibility of featuring them on the menu permanently."

Shelby beamed with pride for her friend. "That's wonderful. Your talent never ceases to amaze me. I'm so proud of you."

"Thanks," Lucy replied, her cheeks flushing with pleasure at the compliment. "But enough about me. How are things at the bookshop? Any interesting new releases or customer stories?"

As they ate, Shelby told Lucy about the day's events, from the excited young reader who had discovered a new favorite series to the eccentric old man who had come in searching for a book on the history of lighthouse keeping.

Shelby said, with a twinkle in her eye, "Mrs. Fitzgerald, the retired librarian, stopped by today. She spent nearly an hour browsing the shelves and telling me stories about her days working at the Hamlet Public Library. It was really interesting."

Lucy smiled, her eyes sparkling with amusement. "That sounds just like Mrs. Fitzgerald. She's a walking encyclopedia of Hamlet history."

As they finished their meal, the two friends cleared the dishes and settled onto the comfortable couch in the living room. Harper, who had been napping in her favorite spot by the window, leaped up to join them, curling contentedly in Shelby's lap.

Shelby stroked the cat's soft fur, feeling a sense of

peace wash over her. "You know, moments like these make me realize just how lucky I am. I have a job I love, wonderful friends like you, this sweet cat, and a home in a town that feels like family."

Lucy smiled. "I feel the same way. I couldn't imagine living anywhere else."

As the conversation shifted to their upcoming drum circle session, Shelby and Lucy discussed the new rhythm they had been learning and the sense of community and connection they felt when playing music with the other participants.

"There's something so cool about drumming together," Shelby mused, her eyes taking on a faraway look. "It's like we're all tapping into an ancient, primal energy that binds us to each other."

Lucy nodded in agreement. "Absolutely. It's a way to express ourselves and communicate without words. Plus, it's just so much fun."

Glancing at the clock, Shelby realized it was time to head to the community center, so she and Lucy got ready to leave.

Harper looked at Shelby and spoke to her mind, "Be careful tonight."

A shiver ran down Shelby's back as she stared at the cat. "Why do you say that?"

"I'm not sure, but I feel something." The feline's tail twitched back and forth.

Lucy knew that Shelby and Harper could communicate with one another. "What's Harper saying?"

"She told us to be careful."

"Why?"

"She isn't sure."

As the two friends stepped out into the busy streets of Hamlet, Shelby took a deep breath, savoring the salty scent of the nearby ocean. The gentle early-August breeze played with her long, wavy hair, and the stars twinkled overhead like a thousand tiny diamonds.

Walking side by side, Shelby and Lucy made their way to the community center, their conversation flowing easily from one topic to another. They reminisced about childhood adventures and laughed at their silly inside jokes.

As they approached the welcoming lights of the community center, Shelby felt a surge of anticipation. She knew the drum circle would be a chance to let go of the day's stresses and connect with friends.

As they entered the warmly lit community center, the rhythmic beating of drums greeted them as a few people practiced. The room was filled with an eclectic mix of people, young and old, all gathered to share their love for music.

On the other side of the circle sat Penny Smith, a new face in Hamlet who had quickly become a regular at the weekly drum sessions. With her long, dark hair that cascaded down her back in loose waves, brown eyes, and infectious smile, Penny stood out like a bright flower. Her slender fingers danced across the surface of her djembe drum, creating intricate patterns that wove seamlessly into the group's collective rhythm.

Shelby and Lucy picked out drums and made their way to the circle, exchanging warm greetings with familiar faces as they settled into their spots. Penny looked up, her eyes sparkling as she spotted her new friends.

"I'm so glad you made it," Penny exclaimed, her voice carrying over the drumming.

Shelby grinned, already feeling the energy of the room wash over her. "We wouldn't miss it."

Lucy nodded in agreement. "I've been looking forward to this all week. It's the perfect way to unwind after a long day baking in the kitchen."

Penny said, "I've been working on a new beat I think you'll like."

As the drumming continued, Shelby found herself falling into the rhythm, her hands moving instinctively over the surface of her drum. She closed her eyes, allowing the music to transport her.

The drum leader walked in and while she got ready to lead the circle, Penny walked over to Shelby and Lucy. "So, what have you two been up to this week? What's new?"

Lucy tucked a stray lock of hair behind her ear. "Well, I've been experimenting with some new pastry recipes at the inn. I'm always on the lookout for fresh flavor combinations for our guests."

Penny's eyes widened with interest. "Oh, that sounds great. I'm not much of a baker. I've always admired people who can create delicious desserts. I did a nice hike in the state park the other day. It was a beautiful trail. It made me relax and feel so peaceful."

Shelby nodded, a smile playing on her lips. "I know exactly what you mean. It's one of the reasons I love living in Hamlet - there's so much to explore right outside our doorstep."

As the conversation flowed, Shelby found herself drawn to Penny's vibrant energy. They knew the newcomer shared many of the same interests as she and Lucy did, from a love of music and the arts to a deep appreciation for the great outdoors.

The drum leader called everyone to form the circle, and she started playing a rhythm. After a few moments, the woman encouraged the participants to join in.

The playing was going well, and Shelby was enjoying the beat until suddenly, as if struck by a bolt of lightning, a heavy sense of unease washed over her. It was a sensation she'd felt before – a subtle tingling at the base of her skull that caused anxiety to fill her veins. Her vision darkened and almost faded as she saw the image of someone entering the community center. Waves of negative energy spilled from the person, and then the hallucination faded.

Shelby's rose quartz pendant grew warm against her skin, and she knew without a doubt that her intuition was trying to tell her something. The necklace was a family heirloom that had been presented to her by her mother and grandmother.

She squared her shoulders, trying to shake off the feeling, but it persisted, nagging at the edges of her consciousness.

Lucy, ever attuned to her friend's moods, leaned in closer. "Are you all right? You look a little pale."

Shelby forced a smile, not wanting to worry her friend. "Uh, yeah," she replied, shaking off the sensation. "I just got lost in the beat for a second."

Even as the words left her lips, Shelby knew the brief flashes of intuition hinted at something lurking beneath the surface. She couldn't quite put her finger on it, but she had a nagging feeling that something was very wrong. Pushing the unsettling thoughts aside, Shelby focused on the present moment, the joy she felt with her friends, and the music that surrounded them.

As the drum circle came to a close, everyone lingered, chatting and enjoying the snacks before they helped pack up the instruments. Shelby, Lucy, and Penny made plans for a hike the next day and set a time and place to meet.

Hugging her friends goodbye, Shelby made her way home through the streets of Hamlet and felt the nagging sensation of unease still tugging at her and making her stomach feel sick.

She knew something was sitting just beneath the surface, waiting to be uncovered.

And she knew it was nothing good.

2

The late afternoon sun cast a pretty light over the town of Hamlet, as Shelby and Lucy laced up their hiking boots in anticipation of their hike with Penny. They were eager to hike an area of the forest where the trail led to a small waterfall. They'd packed swimsuits in their backpacks, in case they wanted to take a dip in the pond beneath the falls.

Harper listened to the conversation from her perch on the wide windowsill.

"Penny's really going to love this hike. I can't wait for us to show her the trail," Lucy said, filling her water bottle at the sink. Her blonde hair was pulled back into a ponytail, and her eyes sparkled.

"Me, too," Shelby replied, adjusting her pendant. The rose quartz stone glimmered in the sunlight, a constant source of comfort and protection. "She's going to love the way the sunlight filters through the trees and the sound of the waterfall ... it's like something out of a fairy tale."

As they waited for Penny to arrive, Harper stood up on the windowsill and said to Shelby's mind, "I have a feeling something's wrong."

Before Shelby could respond to the cat, her phone buzzed with an incoming text message and her eyes narrowed as she read the words on the screen, concern etching lines across her face.

"Hey, what's the matter?" Lucy asked, immediately sensing her friend's unease. She set down her water bottle and moved closer to Shelby, her voice filled with worry.

Shelby answered softly, "Penny says she's feeling really ill and won't be able to join us today."

"Aw, poor thing," Lucy said sympathetically. "I hope she feels better soon. Did she say what's wrong?"

"No, just that she's not feeling well," Shelby replied, a frown tugging at the corners of her mouth.

"It's not like Penny to cancel plans last minute like this," Lucy pointed out. "She's always so energetic and excited about our hikes. She must really feel awful if she canceled."

Shelby agreed, but as she tucked her phone back into her backpack, that same tingling sensation from the drum circle returned – even stronger than before. It was as if an invisible force was trying to tell her something, a nagging feeling that wouldn't go away. She absently rubbed her pendant, the smooth stone warming beneath her fingers.

"What are you thinking? Did you just have some sort of premonition?" Lucy inquired, noticing her friend's distant expression. She was aware of Shelby's paranormal abilities and knew her well enough to recognize when something was bothering her. "You look like you've seen a ghost."

"Something doesn't feel right," Shelby admitted, her eyes clouded with worry. "I think we should go check on Penny. I just ... I have this feeling that there's more to this than just a simple illness." She glanced at Harper, and asked, "Do you sense something?"

"I've sensed unease all day."

"Are we in danger?"

Harper didn't answer right away, but then her tail flicked. "No, but Penny's illness is serious."

"Harper thinks Penny's illness is serious," Shelby told her friend.

"Okay." Lucy nodded. "I hope you're both wrong,

but let's go see how she's doing. Why don't we grab some soup and tea from the café on the way and surprise her with a little care package? That always makes me feel better when I'm under the weather."

The two friends quickly changed out of their hiking boots and headed to the café and bakery on Main Street. The aroma of freshly baked bread and aromatic spices greeted them as they entered, and the friendly barista, Chad, waved at them from behind the counter.

"Hey, Shelby. Hi, Lucy," Chad called out, his warm smile reaching his hazel eyes. "What can I get for you today? The usual?"

"Hi, Chad," Shelby replied, returning his smile. "Actually, we need a large container of your chicken noodle soup and a cup of the soothing herbal tea blend. Our friend Penny is feeling under the weather."

"Oh, no. I hope she feels better soon," Chad said, his face etched with genuine concern. "I'll whip up a special blend just for her - it's my mom's secret recipe for chasing away colds. Works like a charm every time."

As Chad busied himself preparing the care package, Shelby and Lucy chatted quietly, their worry for Penny growing with each passing moment. They knew how much Penny loved their weekly hikes and how excited she'd been to explore the new trail with them.

"I just can't shake this feeling that there's something more going on," Shelby confided, her voice barely above a whisper. "It's like my intuition is warning me about something, but I can't quite put my finger on what it is."

Lucy listened. "You have to pay attention to your intuition. If you think there's more to this, I don't doubt your feelings."

With the soup and tea securely packed, Shelby and Lucy made their way to Penny's modest rental cottage on the outskirts of town. The small, white house was surrounded by a well-tended garden bursting with colorful flowers and fragrant herbs.

As they approached the front door, they noticed it was slightly ajar. Exchanging worried glances, they cautiously entered, calling out Penny's name.

"Penny? It's Shelby and Lucy," Shelby called out, her voice echoing in the quiet house. The normally inviting space felt strangely cold and lifeless, as if the walls were holding their breath.

"Over here," came a weak voice from the living room. There, they found Penny curled up on the couch, her normally vibrant eyes now glassy and feverish. Her brown hair was damp with sweat, and her freckled skin was alarmingly pale.

"Hey, Penny," Shelby said gently, setting the care package on the coffee table. "We brought you some soup and tea. We were worried when you said you weren't feeling well."

"Thanks," Penny whispered, attempting a weak smile as she gratefully accepted the steaming mug of tea from Lucy's hands. Her fingers trembled as she lifted the mug to her lips, taking a cautious sip.

"Has this ever happened before? Could you have food poisoning?" Lucy asked softly, taking in her friend's fragile state. She perched on the edge of the couch, her hand resting comfortingly on Penny's leg.

"No, never," Penny replied, shivering despite the warm blanket wrapped around her shoulders. "It just came on so suddenly last night after the drum circle. I've never felt this sick before."

Shelby's heart clenched at the sight of her friend in such distress. She knew there was more to Penny's illness than met the eye. As she looked at the young woman's face, a chill ran down her spine, and her heart sank.

"Maybe it's just a nasty bug," Lucy suggested, trying to sound optimistic despite the growing concern in her heart.

"Maybe..." Shelby trailed off, her intuition tugging urgently at her thoughts. She glanced down at her pendant, which seemed to pulse with a gentle warmth, urging her to trust her instincts. Taking a deep breath, she turned to face Lucy, her expression grave.

"Listen," she said hesitantly, "I think there's more to this than just a bug. I can't explain it, but I have a feeling something isn't right."

Penny was barely able to keep her eyes open. Her athletic frame had conquered many a hiking trail but now, she was frail and shivering despite the warmth of her home. "Good heavens," Lucy gasped. "Penny, can you hear us?"

The pendulum of Shelby's intuition swung wildly. As she knelt beside Penny, her friend's energy felt chaotic and weakening, a stark contrast to the usually strong and stable person she'd come to know. It was clear that Penny's illness was not just a simple case of the sniffles; this was something far more alarming.

"This is serious," Lucy whispered, the sunny optimism of her nature overshadowed by the gravity of the situation.

"I know," Shelby replied, stroking Penny's hair back from her clammy forehead. "We have to get her to the hospital, now." Shelby's voice was firm as she assessed Penny's pallid face.

Without hesitation, Lucy nodded, her hands trembling.

With a voice that was steady and reassuring, Shelby said, "I think we need to get you to the hospital; get you checked out. Maybe they can give you an IV to be sure you're not getting dehydrated. Better to go and have them examine you than to wait and have you get worse. No need to take any risks."

Penny nodded weakly, her eyes brimming with tears. "I'm scared. I feel so horrible."

"They'll take care of you at the hospital, and you'll be back on your feet in no time," Shelby assured the young woman.

The two friends helped Penny to her feet, supporting her weight as they made their way to the door. Shelby's mind raced with questions and fears. She knew her intuition had been trying to warn her about this very thing.

Together, Shelby and Lucy held Penny's arms from either side, guiding her unsteady steps out of the house and into the warm air that did nothing to revive their friend's vitality. The scent of pine and earth, usually so grounding, seemed inconsequential as they carefully lowered Penny into the backseat of Shelby's car.

"Everything's going to be all right, Penny," Lucy assured softly while fastening the seatbelt around her.

"Keep talking to her, Lucy," Shelby suggested as she slid behind the wheel and gave a silent prayer for protection. She started the engine and reversed out of the driveway.

As they drove to the hospital, Shelby was filled with the nagging feeling that Penny's illness was just the beginning of something much larger. *Please*, she thought. *Please let Penny be okay.*

The drive to the hospital was a blur of motion and emotion. While Shelby navigated the winding roads of Hamlet, the car's interior was thick with tension, punctuated only by Lucy's gentle murmurs of reassurance and the shallow breaths of their stricken friend.

"She's so cold," Lucy said, her hands rubbing Penny's hands and arms in a futile attempt to warm her. "Hold on, Penny."

"I'm doing my best. We'll be there soon," Shelby replied, her eyes never leaving the road as she pressed a little harder on the pedal.

The hospital drew nearer while the sun began to

set over Hamlet, and as they pulled into the hospital parking lot, Shelby knew that something dark had crept into their midst, and it was going to pull them into it.

With a deep breath, she stepped out of the car to help Lucy lift Penny out of the backseat. The young woman's complexion had turned a frightening shade of ashen gray.

As they walked through the hospital doors, with Shelby on one side of Penny and Lucy on the other, the buzzing energy of the emergency room hit them like a wave. Nurses moved deftly between curtained areas, doctors' orders punctuated the air, and the beeping of monitors played a steady, unsettling rhythm.

A nurse with kind eyes and a no-nonsense expression quickly approached, her practiced gaze taking in Penny's condition in an instant. "What happened?" she asked while gesturing for a gurney.

"We don't know," Shelby managed to say, her intuition sending icy pricks down her spine. She wondered fleetingly if this was another premonition or just the cold grip of dread. "She felt sick this morning and got worse throughout the day."

"Let's get her back, stat," the nurse commanded,

her directive summoning a team that materialized to whisk Penny away.

Lucy and Shelby followed as closely as they were allowed before being stopped at the double doors leading to the treatment area. The two friends stood shoulder to shoulder, peering through the small windows of the swinging doors, watching as IV lines were placed and vials of blood drawn. They could see Penny's chest rise and fall, too fast and too shallow, until the medical staff pushed the gurney around a corner and out of sight.

"She's going to be okay, isn't she?" Lucy turned to her friend, searching her face for the reassurance that normally came so easily to both of them.

"I sure hope so."

Time stretched and contracted, playing tricks on their senses. The waiting room became their entire world. They were outsiders here, unable to do more than offer silent support, but they knew their presence mattered.

"Hey, remember the last hike we took with Penny? The one where she insisted on taking the steepest trail?" Lucy's attempt at lightness felt fragile in the clinical air, but it was a lifeline all the same.

Shelby smiled faintly. "Yeah, she said it was the

only way to really experience the woods. 'No path too tough for Penny Smith,'" she mimicked fondly.

"Exactly," Lucy agreed, a tearful chuckle escaping her. "That's why she's going to pull through."

They lapsed into silence again, watching as a nurse finally approached them. "Are you here for Ms. Smith?" the nurse asked, her expression giving away nothing.

"Yes, we're her friends," Shelby replied, her throat tight.

"Please come with me." The nurse gestured toward a small consultation room.

Shelby and Lucy followed, their steps heavy with worry but hopeful their friend was surely fighting her way back through the haze of illness.

3

The tension in the small consultation room was palpable as Shelby and Lucy sat side by side. The sterile white walls and the faint beeping of machines from nearby rooms only added to the sense of unease that hung in the air. They had been waiting for what felt like an eternity, desperate for any news about Penny's condition.

Shelby's mind raced with possibilities, trying to make sense of what had happened to her friend, but try as she might, she couldn't recall anything out of the ordinary except for feeling anxious and uneasy at the drum circle.

Lucy was uncharacteristically quiet. Her eyes were fixed on the door, as if she could will the doctor to appear and give them the answers they so desperately needed.

Finally, after what seemed like hours, the door opened, and a tall, middle-aged man in a white coat entered the room. His face was serious, his eyes tired behind wire-rimmed glasses.

"Shelby Price and Lucy Blake?" he asked, glancing down at the chart in his hands.

"Yes, that's us," Shelby said, rising to her feet. "How is Penny?"

The doctor sighed, running a hand through his graying hair. "I'm afraid I have some troubling news. After running a series of tests, we believe that Penny probably has been infected with anthrax."

Shelby and Lucy exchanged horrified looks, their faces paling at the doctor's words. Anthrax? How was that even possible?

"Anthrax?" Lucy echoed, her voice barely above a whisper. "But how? Where could she have been exposed to something like that?"

The doctor shook his head. "We're not sure at this point. It's an extremely rare infection, and it's not something we see often, especially in a small town like Hamlet. More tests have to be done to be sure, but the authorities have been contacted, and they'll be launching an investigation to determine the probable source of the exposure."

Shelby's mind was reeling. She thought of the shadowy figure she had seen in her vision and the sense of malevolence that had surrounded the person. Could he or she have been responsible for this?

"Is Penny going to be okay?" Shelby asked, almost afraid to hear the answer.

The doctor's expression was grave. "Her condition is poor, but stable for now. We've started her on a course of powerful antibiotics, and we're doing everything we can to support her body's natural defenses. The next few days will be critical."

Lucy's eyes filled with tears. "Can we see her?"

The doctor shook his head sympathetically. "I'm sorry, but Penny is in isolation right now. Until we know more about how she was exposed and ensure that there's no risk of further contamination, we can't allow any visitors."

Shelby's heart sank. The thought of Penny lying alone in a hospital bed, fighting for her life, was almost too much to bear.

"I know this is difficult," the doctor said softly, "but the best thing you can do for Penny right now is to go home and get some rest. We'll keep you updated on any changes in her condition." He looked from one young woman to another. "Have either of you developed any flu-like symptoms?"

Shelby's eyes widened, understanding the doctor's implication. "No, I feel fine."

"So do I." Lucy looked fearful.

"Come back to the emergency room right away, if you start to have any symptoms in the next day or so," the doctor told them. "For now, go home and get some rest."

Shelby and Lucy nodded numbly, knowing there was nothing more they could do at the hospital. As they stood to leave, Lucy remembered the small bag she had been clutching.

"Doctor, this is Penny's wallet. It has her medical insurance information and her parents' contact details. We thought you might need it."

The doctor took the wallet with a grateful nod. "Thank you. We'll make sure to reach out to her family and keep them informed."

With heavy hearts, Shelby and Lucy left the hospital, the bright lights in the parking lot a stark contrast to the dark shadows that had settled over them.

The drive back to Shelby's apartment was silent

for half the trip, each woman lost in her own thoughts.

"Have we been infected with anthrax?" Lucy asked quietly.

"I don't think so, but we'll watch for symptoms over the next twenty-four hours. Shall I drop you off at your place?" Shelby asked her friend.

"Yes, please. I'm exhausted."

In front of her apartment building, Lucy gave Shelby a tight hug. "Try to get some sleep," she said softly. "I know it won't be easy, but we need to stay strong. Penny's going to need us when she wakes up."

Shelby nodded, fighting back a few tears that threatened to fall. "I know. Thanks, Lucy. For everything."

"You, too. Thank heavens we were together." With a final squeeze of Shelby's hand, Lucy left, promising to check in first thing in the morning.

As Shelby entered the space above the bookshop, she felt a wave of exhaustion wash over her. The events of the past hours had taken a toll, both physically and emotionally.

Alone in her apartment, she collapsed onto the couch, her mind still spinning with unanswered questions. Harper, sensing her distress, leaped up beside her, offering a comforting purr.

"How could this have happened, Harper?" Shelby whispered, stroking the cat's soft fur. "Anthrax? It's unbelievable."

Harper had no answers, but the steady rumble of her purr and the warmth of her presence provided Shelby with comfort. "It'll be okay. Penny is fit and strong. She'll get through this."

Despite her exhaustion, sleep eluded Shelby that night. Every time she closed her eyes, images of Penny's pale, stricken face flooded her mind. She tossed and turned, her heart heavy with worry and fear.

As the first light of dawn began to filter through the curtains, Shelby knew she couldn't wait any longer. She reached for her phone, her fingers scrolling through her contacts until she found the one she was looking for: Detective Travis Whitely.

Travis answered on the second ring, his voice rough with sleep. "Shelby? Is everything okay?"

Shelby took a deep breath, trying to steady her racing heart. "Travis, Penny is in the hospital. The doctors say she's been infected with anthrax."

There was a moment of stunned silence on the other end of the line. Then, Travis's voice came through, now fully alert. "We were contacted last night about it. They weren't positive it was anthrax at the time. Are they sure about it?"

"Pretty sure," Shelby said, her voice trembling slightly. "They've run tests, but they need to do more to be certain. I think this might be connected to the vision I had at the drum circle the other night. The shadowy figure, the sense of evil. I think the person could be responsible for this."

Travis's voice was grim. "I've been assigned to the case, Shelby. I'll be leading the investigation into the poisoning. I promise you, we'll get to the bottom of this."

Shelby felt a flicker of hope at Travis's words. If anyone could unravel the mystery and bring Penny's attacker to justice, it was him.

"Thank you," she said softly. "I'm glad you're the one in charge."

Travis replied, "Listen, why don't you come down to the station later today? We can go over everything you remember from the drum circle and see if there are any details that might help us track down who is responsible for the poisoning. It is possible the anthrax came from something within the building, but until we know more, we're treating this as an intentional poisoning."

Shelby agreed, feeling a sense of purpose settle over her. She might not have been able to protect Penny from whomever had targeted her, but she could do everything in her power to help find the person responsible.

As she ended the call, Shelby reached for the pendant that hung around her neck, drawing strength from its gentle energy.

"Hold on, Penny," she whispered, her eyes closing in a silent prayer. "We're going to find out what happened."

It was early evening when Shelby went to meet Detective Whitely at the police station. He smiled brightly when he saw her in the lobby.

"How are you doing?" he asked.

"I'm okay. Still shocked about it all," Shelby admitted.

"Come on, let's go to my office to talk." Once in the office, Travis gestured for her to take a seat as he grabbed a file folder from his desk.

"It's still early, but so far we have a few potential leads," he said, opening the file. "Penny's ex-boyfriend, Brent Collins, seems like the most obvious suspect. Apparently they had a messy breakup a few months back."

Shelby nodded, recalling what Penny had once told her about Brent and his temper. "But she isn't from around here. She last lived in Colorado and just moved to Hamlet. Did he follow her here?"

"It seems he's in the area on vacation."

"Really? That's a strange coincidence, isn't it? He does seem like someone you should look at. Do you know if he made any threats after they split?" Shelby asked.

"Not that we know of yet," Travis replied. "But we're digging deeper into their relationship history as well as his alibi for the night she was poisoned."

The detective flipped through a few pages. "I also spoke with someone at the school where Penny is working. A coworker seems to hold a grudge against her. I need to meet with her."

"I had no idea about that," Shelby said, shaking her head.

Travis went on. "We're also looking into some suspicious individuals seen near the community center around the time Penny would have been attending the drum circle."

He showed Shelby a police sketch of a man in a hoodie lurking by the building. "Ring any bells?"

Shelby studied it closely but couldn't place the face. "No, I don't recognize him. I didn't get any odd vibes from strangers last night."

"We'll keep digging on that front," Travis said. He closed the file, looking at Shelby intently. "There was a case in New Hampshire not long ago where a young woman was infected with anthrax after the drum's skin had been replaced. We've closed the community center and are investigating if any of the drum heads have been replaced recently."

Shelby tilted her head to the side. "Are you thinking the drum itself infected Penny?"

"It's a possibility. Does your intuition tell you anything about this case?" Travis asked.

Shelby closed her eyes, concentrating deeply to see if any impressions came to her. She took a slow, deep breath as she focused her mind, trying to tap into any intuitive senses about the poisoning. Flashes of imagery and emotion flickered through her thoughts.

She saw Penny laughing at the drum circle, filled with happiness. Then a shift - Penny looked fearful, clutching her chest in pain. Another flash showed the community center entrance, a shadowy figure slipping inside unseen. Negative energy radiated from the person, making Shelby shiver.

Her eyes opened. "I'm getting the sense this was personal, that someone wanted to hurt Penny specifically. It wasn't random or opportunistic."

Travis nodded, scribbling notes. "That matches our thinking, too. This was planned and targeted."

Shelby went on. "While we were all drumming, I had a vision of a shadowy person entering the building during the day. They might be the one who poisoned her drum."

"Can you describe the person at all?" Travis asked.

Shelby tried to recall details, but the figure remained obscured. "Not really. I think the hair was light and a little longer than most men wear it. He was wearing a baseball cap. I sensed a feeling of bad will coming off him." Her eyes narrowed. "Although, the person could be a woman who had her hair pulled up in a loose bun. Do you have any suspects like that, who might be involved with changing out the drum?"

Travis flipped through some files. "Maybe. We're still building our suspect pool. We'll see if any of them seem to match your impression."

He smiled at Shelby. "This is really helpful. We'll get to the bottom of this. Will you be able to help out now and then?"

"I'd be glad to help." Shelby returned the smile, glad to lend her talents to the investigation. She wanted to find who hurt her friend and make sure no one else was in danger.

"I'm going to follow up with Penny's ex first thing tomorrow," Travis said. "Want to join me?"

"Definitely," Shelby replied. "Let's find out what he's been up to."

4

It was a hot and humid day as Detective Travis Whitely and Shelby pulled up to a resort of quaint cottages on the outskirts of Hamlet. The historic main building, with its white clapboard siding and black shutters, seemed to belong to a different era, a time when life was simpler and the world less complicated.

But as Shelby stepped out of Travis's car, she had the feeling the idyllic setting was merely a façade, hiding a darker truth that might lay beneath the surface. They were there to interview Brent Collins, Penny's ex-boyfriend, who had recently arrived in town for a two-week vacation with his new girlfriend, Sandy Wills.

Travis led the way up the gravel path to cottage

number five, his broad shoulders squared with determination, and Shelby followed close behind. She had never met Brent, but from what Penny had told her, their relationship had been tumultuous at best.

As they reached the front door, Travis paused, turning to face her.

"Remember, we're just here to get information," he said, his blue eyes locking with hers. "We don't have anything solid on Brent yet, so let's keep an open mind and see what he has to say."

Shelby nodded, taking a deep breath to steady her nerves. She knew that Travis was right, but she was experiencing a sense of unease about the whole situation.

Travis knocked on the door, the sound echoing through the quiet surroundings. A moment later, it swung open, revealing a tall, athletic man with close-cropped blond hair and piercing green eyes. Brent Collins.

"Oh, hello, you must be the detective," he said, his voice smooth and confident.

Travis flashed his badge. "Detective Travis Whitely, Hamlet PD. This is Shelby Price, my assistant."

"Come in," Brent told them.

The interior of the cottage was just as charming and rustic as the outside, with a few pieces of antique furniture and floral wallpaper creating a homey atmosphere, but Shelby couldn't focus on the décor. Her attention was fixed solely on Brent.

"This is my girlfriend Sandy Wills." Brent gestured to a petite, athletic woman who emerged from the kitchen. Sandy's pretty eyes were set in a delicate face framed by her soft blonde hair, her warmth evident as her lips curved into a welcoming grin.

"Nice to meet you both," Sandy said, extending a hand first to Shelby, then to Travis. Her grip was firm, her demeanor one of kindness that contrasted with Brent's more aloof manner.

"Likewise," Travis replied, his detective's gaze sweeping the room, missing no detail.

Shelby felt a wave of something pass over her, a whisper of something unspoken that lingered in the space between polite greetings and the unsaid questions that hung in the air. She wondered what information might be found when talking to the couple.

Shelby shared a subtle glance with the detective, and their eyes locked for a moment, wordlessly conveying the weight of suspicion that hung between them. Her intuition hummed with an undercurrent of unease, suggesting that things were not as tranquil as they appeared.

"Quite the nice spot you picked for a getaway," Travis remarked. His voice was easy, tinged with genuine admiration for the natural beauty that surrounded the cottages.

Brent shifted back in his chair, the wood creaking slightly under his athletic frame. "Yeah, it's perfect for some peace and quiet. Just what we needed."

"It's always nice to have an escape from the hustle and bustle," Shelby added. "Have you had a chance to do any hiking? The trails around here are really breathtaking this time of year."

Sandy's eyes lit up with enthusiasm. "Oh, we've explored quite a bit. The trails are beautiful. It's like stepping into another world where you can just ... breathe."

The detective said, "As you know, we're here to ask you a few questions about Penny Smith."

At the mention of Penny's name, Brent's face remained impassive. "So, what's this about Penny? I haven't seen her in months."

Travis's elbows rested on his knees. "Penny was poisoned with anthrax two nights ago at the community center. She's in critical condition at the hospital."

Brent's eyebrows shot up, but his expression remained neutral. "Anthrax? That's terrible. Will she be all right?"

Shelby couldn't help but notice the lack of concern in Brent's voice. If he ever cared about Penny, wouldn't he be more upset by the news of her poisoning?

"It's still touch and go. We're trying to piece together what happened," Travis said, his tone even.

"Can you tell us where you were two nights ago?"

Brent shrugged. "I was on a night hike with Sandy. We wanted to explore some of the trails around here; see the stars without all the light pollution. What happened to Penny doesn't have anything to do with me."

Shelby's intuition prickled. A night hike? It seemed like the perfect alibi, but something about Brent's demeanor felt off.

"Can anyone confirm that?" Travis asked, jotting down notes in his small leather-bound notebook.

Brent nodded. "Sandy, of course. And we ran into a couple of other hikers on the trail. I didn't catch their names, but I'm sure they'd remember us."

Travis made a few more notes, his pen scratching

against the paper. "And how would you describe your relationship with Penny? I understand you two used to date."

Brent crossed his ankle over his knee. "We did, but that was over months ago. Things just didn't work out between us. Different priorities, you know?"

Shelby couldn't stay silent any longer. "Penny mentioned that your breakup was pretty rough. That there were a lot of arguments and hard feelings."

Brent's eyes flashed with annoyance, but he quickly masked it with a smile. "Break-ups are never easy, but that's ancient history. I've moved on, and I assume Penny has, too."

The way Brent spoke about Penny, as if she were a distant memory, made Shelby's skin crawl. How could he be so cavalier when she was fighting for her life in the hospital?

The detective asked, "Do you know if Penny had any enemies?"

Something passed over Brent's face, but whatever it was, it was gone in a flash. "I really don't know. Like I said, I haven't seen her in a long time."

"When you were together, was she ever worried about someone?" Travis prodded.

Brent shrugged. "Not to my knowledge."

"Did she ever get any threatening calls or notes?"

Brent shook his head. "She never told me, if she did."

After more questions, Detective Whitely, sitting across from Brent, cleared his throat—a subtle signal that it was time to conclude their visit. He offered a courteous nod, his dark brown eyes meeting Brent's squarely.

"Thank you both for your time today," he said smoothly. "We may have more questions for you later, so please don't leave town without notifying us. Your cooperation is appreciated, and it's important we gather all the details to piece together what happened to Penny."

Shelby rose, and Brent stood as well, his tall frame towering over her. "Of course. I hope Penny makes a full recovery. We understand how serious this is, and we're happy to help in any way we can."

But as they shook hands, Shelby noticed that Brent hadn't asked much of anything about Penny's condition or prognosis. It was as if he didn't care at all.

"Hamlet may be small, but we look out for one another here," Shelby said warmly, her gaze shifting between Brent and Sandy. "We all want to see Penny healthy and thriving again."

"Absolutely," Sandy echoed, her eyes seeming to show genuine concern. It seemed more than mere politeness.

"Enjoy the rest of your stay," Shelby concluded, offering them a reassuring smile. She and Detective Whitely made their way to the door, the detective's broad shoulders casting a protective shadow as they stepped onto the porch.

"Take care," Brent called out after them, his voice carrying a hint of something—was it relief, or maybe apprehension?

As they stepped back out into the bright sunlight, Shelby turned to Travis. "He's hiding something. I can feel it."

Travis nodded. "I agree. His story about the night hike will have to be checked out, but there's definitely more to it than he's letting on."

They walked back to the car, each lost in their own thoughts. As Travis started the engine, his phone buzzed with an incoming text. "Penny's parents just arrived at the hospital. They want to talk to us."

He showed the message to Shelby, who nodded grimly. "Let's go. Maybe they can shed some light on Penny's relationship with Brent."

As they drove away from the rustic resort, Shelby

had the feeling they were only scratching the surface of the mystery surrounding Penny's poisoning. She wondered if Brent was involved somehow, but she knew proving it would be another matter entirely.

They arrived at the hospital just as Penny's parents were leaving the ICU. Mrs. Smith, a petite woman with the same shade of brown hair as her daughter, was leaning heavily on her husband's arm, her face streaked with tears.

"Mr. and Mrs. Smith?" Travis called out, approaching the couple with Shelby close behind. "I'm Detective Whitely, and this is Shelby Price. I'm investigating Penny's case."

Mr. Smith, a tall, broad-shouldered man with kind eyes, shook Travis's hand. "Thank you, Detective. We appreciate everything you're doing to find out who did this to our daughter."

Mrs. Smith sniffed, dabbing at her eyes with a crumpled tissue. "Please, call us John and Mary. Penny always speaks so highly of you, Shelby. She considers you one of her close friends."

Shelby felt a lump form in her throat at Mary's words. "Penny is a wonderful person. The detective is doing everything he can to get to the bottom of this."

John nodded, his face etched with worry. "The doctors say she's stable for now, but the next forty-eight hours will be critical. We just don't understand how this could have happened."

Travis cleared his throat. "That's actually why we wanted to speak with you. We're trying to piece together Penny's relationships and any potential conflicts she may have had. Can you tell us about her ex-boyfriend, Brent Collins?"

Mary's face darkened at the mention of Brent's name. "That man..." she said, her voice trembling with anger. "He was no good for Penny. Always trying to control her, to make her into someone she wasn't."

John put a comforting arm around his wife's shoulders. "Penny broke things off with him months ago. It was a difficult decision for her, but she knew it was the right thing to do."

Shelby asked, "Did Brent ever make any threats against Penny? Did he seem like the type of person who might want to hurt her?"

John shook his head. "Not explicitly, no, but there was always something about him that felt off, like he was hiding a darker side beneath that charming exterior."

Mary nodded in agreement. "Penny mentioned that he had a terrible temper; that he would lash out at her over the smallest things. She was always walking on eggshells around him."

Travis made a few notes in his notebook. "And did Penny ever mention a woman named Sandy Wills? Apparently, she's Brent's new girlfriend."

Both John and Mary looked surprised at the mention of Sandy's name. "No, we've never heard of her," John said. "But then again, Penny didn't really like to talk about Brent after their breakup. I think she just wanted to put that whole chapter of her life behind her."

Shelby's mind was racing with this new information. Brent's controlling nature, his terrible temper ... it all pointed to a man who was capable of violence, but without any concrete evidence tying him to the poisoning, they were still grasping at straws.

As they said their goodbyes to John and Mary, promising to keep them updated on any new developments, Shelby had the feeling they might be running out of time. Penny's life hung in the balance, and there was nothing they could do to help her.

Travis must have sensed her distress because as they walked back to the car, he placed a comforting hand on her shoulder. "We'll find the person who did this. I promise you that."

Shelby nodded, trying to draw strength from Travis's words. As they drove back to the station, Shelby's mind was already racing ahead, trying to piece together the clues they had gathered so far. The shadowy figure from her visions, the negative energy that seemed to cling to Brent like a second skin ... it all had to be connected in some way.

But how?

5

The quaint little café on the corner of Main Street was a welcome respite from the chaos and uncertainty that had engulfed Shelby and Detective Whitely over the past few days. As they stepped inside, the aroma of freshly brewed coffee and warm cinnamon rolls washed over them, providing a momentary sense of comfort in the midst of their troubled thoughts.

They had come there to meet with Lena Winthrop, the leader of the drum circle at the community center where Penny might have been poisoned. Shelby and the detective hoped that Lena might be able to shed some light on the events leading up to that fateful night, and perhaps provide a clue that would help them unravel the mystery of who had targeted Penny.

As they scanned the interior of the café, Shelby saw a woman seated at a corner table, her hands wrapped around a steaming mug of tea. In her fifties, Lena Winthrop was a striking figure, with auburn hair that fell around her shoulders.

Shelby led the way over to her table. "Lena, hi."

Lena stood to hug the young woman. "Shelby, it's so good to see you. I can't believe what happened to Penny."

"This is Detective Travis Whitely. He's investigating the case."

Travis showed the badge that was already in his hand. "Hello, Lena. We spoke on the phone earlier about Penny Smith's case."

Lena looked up at him, her eyes filled with a deep sadness that Shelby recognized all too well. It was the same sadness that had haunted her own heart since the moment she had learned of Penny's poisoning.

"Yes, of course. Please, join me," Lena said, gesturing to the empty chairs across from her. "I've been so worried about Penny. How is she doing?"

Shelby and Travis briefly made eye contact before taking their seats.

"She's still in critical condition," Travis said, his voice gentle but firm. "The doctors are doing everything they can, but the next few days will be crucial."

Lena closed her eyes for a moment, as if absorbing the weight of Travis's words. When she opened them again, they were glistening with unshed tears. "I just can't believe this is happening. Penny is such a kind, gentle soul. Who would want to hurt her like this?"

Shelby reached across the table and took Lena's hand in her own, offering a silent gesture of support and understanding. "That's what we're trying to find out. We're hoping you might be able to help us piece together what happened that night."

Lena took a deep, shaky breath before nodding. "Of course. Anything I can do to help."

Travis held his notebook and pen at the ready. "Can you tell us about the drums that were used in the circle that night? Were they the usual ones? Was there anything different about them?"

Lena bit her lip as she thought back to the events of that evening. "Most of the drums were the usual ones we use every week, but now that you mention it, about a week ago, we had some of the drumheads replaced by a man who owns a shop a couple of towns over. He came highly recommended, so we didn't think much of it at the time."

Shelby's intuition prickled at the mention of the drumhead replacements. "Do you know the name of the shop or the owner?"

Lena shook her head. "I'm afraid I don't. One of the other members of the circle handled all the arrangements, but I can ask them for the name." The woman's face brightened. "I think I remember seeing the name of the shop on the man's work case. I believe the shop is in Oakville. To be certain, I'll ask the person who hired the man."

Travis made a note in his book. "That would be very helpful, Lena. And where are the drums stored when they're not in use?"

"In the basement of the community center," Lena replied. "That's where we keep all of our equipment and supplies."

Travis nodded, his mind racing ahead to the next steps in the investigation. "We'd love to take a look at the drums, but the community center is closed to everyone except the investigators from the Massachusetts Department of Environmental Services and other medical experts. It is important that no one else is exposed to the toxin. The drums, as well as the rooms in the center, are being tested for any traces of the anthrax spores."

Lena nodded. "Yes, I understand. They don't know how long the center will be closed."

"Do you know if anyone else had access to the basement besides the members of the circle?"

Lena thought for a moment. "The basement is kept locked when the center is closed, but other instructors use it for equipment storage. Only a few of us have keys though."

Shelby's mind was spinning with possibilities. If someone had tampered with the drums in the basement, it would have to be someone with access to the space. But who would have had a motive to target Penny specifically?

As if reading her thoughts, Travis turned to Lena with a serious expression. "I have to ask. Do you know if Penny has any enemies, anyone who might have wanted to hurt her?"

Lena's eyes widened in surprise. "No, of course not. Everyone likes Penny. She has such a gentle, caring spirit. I can't imagine anyone wanting to cause her harm."

But even as the words left her lips, a flicker of doubt crossed Lena's face. "Although ... there was something that happened a couple of weeks ago. It might not be related, but it was a little unusual."

Shelby's heart pounded. "What was it, Lena?"

The woman hesitated for a moment, as if trying to find the right words. "Someone came to the community center and donated three drums. They're beautiful instruments, hand-crafted and adorned with intricate designs. I wasn't there when the man dropped them off. I only arrived about an hour after he left."

"Donated drums?" Travis repeated, exchanging a look with Shelby.

Lena nodded. "Yes. The person left them right inside the front entrance, along with a note saying they were a gift. The drums weren't labeled with any shop name or anything."

"So you didn't get a look at who donated them?" Shelby clarified.

"No, I'm afraid not," Lena said regretfully. "Whoever it was didn't leave a name. Our director thought it was just someone being generous."

Travis rubbed his chin thoughtfully. The timing of the drum donation seemed suspicious, as did the recent drumhead replacement from the out-of-town shop. Were the two incidents connected?

He met Shelby's gaze, seeing the same realization in her eyes. They now had two solid leads to follow up on.

"When exactly were the drums donated?" Travis asked, his pen poised above his notebook.

"A couple of days before Penny took ill," Lena said, her voice tight with worry. "Do you think they could be connected to what happened to Penny?"

Travis's jaw clenched as he considered the possibilities. "It's too early to say for sure, but it's definitely something we'll need to look into. Does anyone remember anything about the person who donated the drums? What they looked like, what they were wearing?"

Lena said, "I'm sorry, I didn't see him myself, but one of the other circle members mentioned that he was of average height and had dark blond hair. He was wearing a baseball cap, a black jacket, and sunglasses, even though it was cloudy that day."

Shelby felt a chill run down her spine at the description. It was vague, but something they were talking about felt familiar, like a half-remembered dream that danced just out of reach.

Travis finished jotting down the details in his notebook before standing up and offering Lena a reassuring smile. "Thank you, Lena. You've been a big help. We'll let you know if we have any more questions, but in the meantime, please don't hesitate to reach out if you remember anything else."

Lena nodded, her eyes still haunted by the weight of Penny's fate. "Of course. And please, let me know if there's anything else I can do to help. Penny is a valued member of our group."

As Shelby and Travis left the café and stepped out into the bright sunlight, Shelby said, "Now there are two solid leads to follow up on."

"Two very interesting leads." Travis placed a comforting hand on her shoulder as they walked down the sidewalk. "We're getting closer, but we need to be careful. Whoever did this to Penny is still out there."

Shelby nodded, her resolve hardening with every step.

As they continued down the busy streets of town, Shelby's mind was already racing ahead to their next move. They needed to track down the mysterious man who had donated the drums and find out if he had any connection to Penny's poisoning. They also had to contact the man from the drum shop who replaced the drum heads.

She wished they could go into the community center, but the place was off-limits. As they approached the building, they were met with a flurry of activity. Several vehicles from the Massachusetts Department of Environmental Services were parked outside, along with a few unmarked vans that Shelby assumed belonged to other medical experts.

Yellow caution tape cordoned off the entrance, and a stern-looking man in a hazmat suit approached them as they drew near.

"I'm sorry, but the community center is closed to the public," he said, his voice muffled behind his protective gear. "We're conducting a thorough environmental sampling to determine if there has been a contamination."

Travis flashed his badge. "Detective Travis Whitely, Hamlet PD. This is Shelby Price, a consultant on the case. Is there anyone we can speak with about the incident?"

"Of course, Detective. Dr. Elizabeth Donaldson is over there by the white tent. She can answer your questions."

Shelby felt a shiver of apprehension run through her at the thought of donning a hazmat suit and entering the contaminated space and was glad they weren't allowed to go into the building. Despite the buzz of activity, she felt a sense of eerie stillness that seemed to permeate the area.

They made their way over to the tent and introduced themselves to Dr. Donaldson.

"We've already begun sampling the drums," the specialist explained. "So far, we've identified traces of anthrax spores on several of the drumheads, including the one that Penny Smith was using on the night of the poisoning. It's possible that only one drum was initially contaminated, but the spores traveled from that one to others."

Shelby's heart clenched at the confirmation. It was possible someone had deliberately targeted Penny, and they had used the drums as their weapon of choice.

The environmental specialist said, "Three drums had very intricate designs. We've taken samples from all of the drums, but we're particularly interested in these three. They were the most recent additions to the collection."

Shelby wondered if the decorated drums could be the key to unlocking the mystery of Penny's poisoning.

When they finished talking with Dr. Donaldson, Shelby and Travis started away. She turned to him with a determined expression. "We need to find out more about

those three drums; who made them, where they

came from, and why someone went to the trouble of donating them to the circle just days before the poisoning."

Travis nodded, his jaw set in a grim line. "Agreed. I'll put out an APB on the description of the man who dropped them off, and we'll start digging into any possible connections between the drums and Penny's illness."

An idea popped into Shelby's mind. "Maybe Penny wasn't a target at all. Maybe the whole thing was just an accident. One of those new drum heads could have been infected with the anthrax spores, depending on where it came from."

"And the donated drums may have been sitting in someone's attic for decades, or longer," Travis pointed out. "There may be no ill intent at all."

Shelby sighed, shivering slightly. "I have a bad feeling about the drums. My intuition is sending up warning signals. If ill intent was involved, then somewhere out there, a dangerous person is on the loose."

6

It was early evening when Lucy and Shelby bustled around in Lucy's kitchen, where the countertops were laden with baking supplies and utensils.

Lucy stood at the center of it all, her hair pulled back into a messy bun and a determined glint in her eyes. She had spent the morning poring over her recipe books, searching for new and innovative flavor combinations to incorporate into her catering menu.

Beside her, Shelby leaned against the counter, her dark hair falling in soft waves below her shoulders. She had come over to help Lucy brainstorm ideas for expanding her business, and the two friends had been deep in conversation for an hour, their voices rising and falling with excitement.

Harper had come along and was sitting on the wide windowsill alternating between watching what the young women were making and what was going on outside.

"The catering business has a few clients already, but I really want to take Pastry Perfections to the next level," Lucy said, her eyes narrowed in concentration as she measured out flour and sugar into a large mixing bowl. "I know I can handle more. I just need to get my name out there and show people what I'm capable of."

Shelby nodded, her expression full of enthusiasm. "I think a marketing plan is a great idea. We can start by setting up social media pages for your business, and I can help you create a website, too. That way, potential clients can see your work and get in touch with you easily."

Lucy's face lit up at the suggestion, a grin spreading across her face. "That would be amazing. Those are great ideas. Thank you so much for your help."

Shelby waved a hand dismissively. "That's what friends are for. Besides, I have a feeling that once people taste your incredible desserts, they'll be lining up to hire you for their events."

As Lucy began to mix the ingredients together,

the rich scent of vanilla and cinnamon filling the air, Shelby's eyes suddenly widened with an idea.

"Hey, why don't you come to the next event at the bookshop and bring some samples of your work? I'm hosting a talk by a local romance author in a few days, and I bet the audience would love to try your desserts."

Lucy paused, her mixer still whirring as she considered the idea. "Oh, that's a smart suggestion. Since it's a romance-themed event, I could make cupcakes in shades of white, pink, and red. I could decorate them with edible flowers, crystals, and frosting ribbons, like something you might see at a bridal shower or wedding."

Shelby smiled, her eyes shining with excitement. "That's perfect. I can already picture how beautiful they'll look on the refreshment table. And who knows? Maybe some of the guests will be planning their own weddings or showers and will want to hire you to cater their special day."

Lucy's heart swelled with gratitude for her friend, a lump rising in her throat as she realized just how much Shelby believed in her.

As the two friends continued to work side by side in the kitchen, their chuckles and chatter filling the air, Lucy was feeling hopeful about her plans. She loved working as a full-time pastry chef at the high-end bed and breakfast near the common, but still, she wanted her own business. She'd always loved baking; she always found joy in creating something beautiful and delicious from simple ingredients.

But now, with Shelby's encouragement and the prospect of showcasing her talents to a wider audience, Lucy felt like she was finally on the cusp of something big, something that could change her life in ways she'd never imagined.

Together, they spent the afternoon experimenting with new recipes and flavor combinations, their hands moving in a flurry of activity as they mixed and measured, stirred and poured. They made truffles infused with lavender and honey, whose delicate shells gave way to a smooth, creamy interior that melted on the tongue. The floral notes of the lavender were perfectly balanced by the sweet essence of the honey, and each truffle was hand-rolled and dusted with a fine layer of cocoa powder.

They baked cupcakes with swirls of raspberry and dark chocolate, their moist, tender crumb giving way to a burst of bright, tangy fruit. The frosting was a swirl of pale pink and rich chocolate, the two flavors melding together. Each cupcake was topped with a fresh raspberry and a sprinkle of dark chocolate shavings.

The last items they made were muffins with golden, crisp tops that gave way to a soft, fluffy interior packed with flavor and texture. Lucy had experimented with a variety of combinations, from the classic blueberry and lemon to more adventurous pairings like pistachio and cardamom, or fig and goat cheese. Each muffin was a little work of art, studded with plump, juicy fruits or crunchy nuts, and infused with the delicate, aromatic notes of spices and herbs.

As the time ticked by and the kitchen filled with the tantalizing aromas of their creations, Lucy was pleased with her creations but knew she had a long way to go and that building a successful catering business would take time, hard work, and dedication.

She imagined herself in a bustling kitchen surrounded by a team of skilled bakers and assistants, working to create exquisite and decadent desserts, and at glamorous events and sophisticated soirées, her sweets the talk of the town.

When the last batch of muffins emerged from the oven, Lucy and Shelby sat down to sample their creations with cups of tea.

"These are so great. I could eat all of them." Shelby reached for another truffle. "They're going to be big hits."

"I sure hope so." Lucy had a small notebook next to her plate, and as she sampled the new confections, she occasionally made a note about how to improve on the flavor or texture.

When they'd finished the taste tests, the friends moved to the big desk in the living room, where Shelby began the work of building the website. Lucy showed her examples of sites she liked, and Harper kept offering suggestions by speaking to Shelby's mind.

They made good progress on the social media pages and the business site before calling it a night. A few more hours of tweaks were needed, and then everything would be done.

"It's only a matter of time before the jobs come pouring in." Shelby closed her laptop. "I think you giving me twenty percent of what you're paid for each job you get would be fair compensation for my hard work on your behalf."

"Dream on." Lucy playfully elbowed her friend. "You'll be lucky to get a few free pastries."

7

Travis and Shelby pulled up in front of the drum shop, a small brick building nestled between a quaint bookstore and a busy café on the Main Street of Oakville. Lena Winthrop had spoken with the person at the community center who had arranged the drum head replacement, and she called the detective to tell him the name of the shop. The storefront was adorned with a colorful sign that read "Rhythm & Beats" in bold, eye-catching letters.

As they stepped inside, the inviting space greeted them with the rhythmic sounds of drums being played by customers trying out the instruments. The walls were lined with a diverse array of drums from all over the world, each one unique in its shape, size, and design.

A friendly face emerged from behind the counter, a man in his mid-fifties with salt-and-pepper hair and a warm, welcoming smile. He approached Travis and Shelby, extending his hand in greeting.

"Welcome to Rhythm & Beats. I'm Alex Johnson, the owner of this little slice of percussion paradise. How can I help you folks today?"

Travis reached into his pocket and pulled out his badge, introducing himself and Shelby. "Detective Travis Whitely, Hamlet PD, and this is Shelby Price, a consultant working with us. We're here to ask you a few questions about some drum heads you recently replaced for the community center in Hamlet."

Mr. Johnson's smile faltered slightly, concern etching itself onto his features. "Of course, Detective. Please, have a seat," he said, gesturing to a few stools near the counter. "What seems to be the problem?"

Shelby spoke up, her voice gentle but firm. "There's been an incident at the community center, Mr. Johnson. One of the drums was contaminated with anthrax, and a woman named Penny Smith was poisoned as a result."

Mr. Johnson's eyes widened in shock, his face

paling at the news. "Anthrax? My gosh, that's terrible. Is Ms. Smith all right?"

Travis shook his head solemnly. "She's in critical condition at the hospital. We're doing everything we can to find out how this happened and who might be responsible."

The shop owner nodded, his expression grave. "I understand. I replaced the drum heads for the community center about a week ago. They were old and worn, and they wanted to make sure the drums were in top condition for the weekly drum circle. I understand the class is becoming very popular."

Shelby's eyes searched Mr. Johnson's face. "Can you walk us through the process of how you replaced the drum heads? We're trying to determine if there were any opportunities for someone to tamper with them."

Mr. Johnson thought for a moment. "Well, I start by carefully removing the old heads, making sure not to damage the drums themselves. Then, I inspect each drum thoroughly, checking for any cracks, dents, or other issues that might affect the sound quality."

He paused, rubbing his chin thoughtfully. "Once I'm satisfied with the condition of the drums, I select the appropriate replacement heads based on the size and type of each instrument. I always use high-quality materials to ensure the best possible sound and durability."

Travis jotted down notes in his notebook. "And during this process, did you notice anything unusual or out of the ordinary? Any suspicious individuals hanging around the community center?"

Mr. Johnson shook his head, his tone of voice earnest. "No, Detective. I take great pride in my work and my shop. If I had seen anything that raised red flags, I would have reported it immediately."

Shelby glanced around the shop, taking in the rows of gleaming drums and the occasional customer testing out a new instrument. "Mr. Johnson, would you mind if we took a look at any documents or records related to the drum head replacements? Receipts, invoices, anything that might help us track down where the materials came from and who had access to them?"

The shop owner nodded, a look of understanding crossing his face. "Of course, Ms. Price. I keep detailed records of all my work, including the specific materials used for each job. Just give me a moment to gather everything for you."

He disappeared into the back room, leaving Travis and Shelby alone among the drums. Shelby ran her fingers along the smooth surface of a nearby bongo. "What do you think?" she asked Travis. "Could Mr. Johnson be involved somehow?"

Travis shook his head. "I don't think so. He seems genuinely shocked and concerned about what happened to Penny. If he wanted to harm someone, why go through the trouble of replacing the drum heads himself? It would be much easier to tamper with them after the fact."

Shelby nodded, seeing the logic in Travis's words. "You're right, but if Mr. Johnson isn't involved, then who had access to the drums long enough to put the toxin on one of them? How did they manage to contaminate the drums without anyone noticing?"

Before Travis could respond, Mr. Johnson returned, a stack of papers in his hands. He placed them on the counter, spreading them out for Travis and Shelby to examine.

"Here you go. Here's everything related to the drum head replacement, including the invoice for the materials and a detailed log of the work I performed."

Travis and Shelby read over the documents, their eyes scanning for any clues or discrepancies. Everything seemed to be in order, from the receipts for the drum heads to the meticulously kept records of Mr. Johnson's work.

After several minutes, Travis looked up. "Thank you, Mr. Johnson. This is all very helpful. We appreciate your cooperation in our investigation."

Mr. Johnson nodded, a sad smile on his face. "Of course, Detective. I want to do everything I can to help find out who did this to Ms. Smith. It breaks my heart to think of her suffering like this."

Shelby nodded. "You've been very helpful. Detective Whitely and the other investigators are doing all they can to find the person responsible."

The shop owner said, "Thank you, Ms. Price. I'm glad to hear it, and I'm sure it will mean even more to Ms. Smith and her loved ones." The man's face suddenly took on a look of worry. "Am I in danger? I worked closely on the drums and I spent a lot of time in the basement of the community center. Could I have come in contact with the anthrax?"

"If you had, you would have most certainly developed symptoms by now," the detective told him. "You're in the clear."

"Thank heavens," the man sighed.

As they left the drum shop, Travis and Shelby walked in silence for a few moments, each lost in their own thoughts. Finally, Shelby spoke up, her voice soft but determined.

"So, if Mr. Johnson isn't involved, where do we go from here? We're running out of leads. There's the woman who Penny reported for wrongdoing, and there's the man who donated the drums, but how will you ever find him?"

Travis sighed, his broad shoulders slumping slightly under the weight of the investigation. "We keep digging. We follow up on every possible lead, no matter how small or insignificant it might seem. We talk to Penny's friends, her family, her colleagues, or anyone who might have had a motive or a grudge against her. And we try to find out who the mystery man who donated the drums is. Someone must know who he is."

Shelby nodded. "You're right. There's still a lot to be done."

As they climbed into Travis's car and pulled away from the drum shop, Shelby felt they were missing something, some crucial piece of information that would unlock the mystery of Penny's poisoning.

She glanced over at Travis, taking in the determined set of his jaw and the intensity in his eyes. She knew he would do everything he could to find the truth, and she felt a surge of gratitude and affection for the man beside her.

"Thank you," she said softly, her hand resting lightly on his arm. "For everything. I wouldn't know what to do if you weren't involved."

Travis looked over at her, a small smile on his lips. "We'll figure it out. With my investigative experience and your intuition, the perp doesn't stand a chance."

As the sun began to set over the quiet town, casting long shadows across the streets, Shelby knew that the work was really just beginning.

8

The weather was clear with no humidity as the sun headed toward the horizon and sent a lovely light over the sprawling gardens of the clifftop mansion where the hospital fundraiser was taking place. The air was warm and sweet, filled with the scent of blooming flowers and the gentle murmur of conversation as guests mingled and laughed beneath the white tents that dotted the lawn.

Shelby and Lucy moved through the crowd, their light pink aprons emblazoned with the words "Pastry Perfections" in elegant magenta script. Like a well-oiled machine, they worked seamlessly together to ensure the pastries and desserts were perfect.

For Lucy, this was more than just another catering gig. It was a chance to showcase her talents, to prove to the wealthy and influential guests that she could provide high-end products that were both delicious and beautifully presented. She had poured her heart and soul into every bite-sized morsel, every delicate buttercream rose, and now, as she watched the guests sample her creations with delight and amazement, she felt a swell of pride and satisfaction that made all the long hours and hard work feel worthwhile.

Shelby, too, was in her element. She loved the energy and excitement of events like this, the chance to meet new people and enjoy the atmosphere of luxury and refinement. As she moved through the crowd, offering trays laden with Lucy's exquisite pastries, she felt proud and happy for her friend. Returning to the pastry display table to replenish her tray, she admired the way Lucy had set up the table.

There were several levels of presentation with pastries arranged on platters and three-tiered servers with vases of flowers mixed in, along with layers of light pink and green fabric wound around the serving plates. The display was elegant, refined, and stylish.

"Shelby, have you tried these mini chocolate truffles?" Lucy asked, pointing to a platter of the decadent treats. "I used a new recipe, and I'm dying to know what you think."

Shelby popped one of the truffles into her mouth, letting the rich, velvety chocolate melt on her tongue. "Oh my gosh, Lucy," she moaned, her eyes closed in bliss. "These are incredible. The hint of sea salt really brings out the sweetness of the chocolate. You've outdone yourself, as usual."

Lucy beamed at the praise, her cheeks flushing with pride. "Thanks. I was nervous about trying something new here, but I'm so glad it paid off. I really want to impress these guests and show them what I can do. If they like my desserts, it could lead to new jobs catering their events."

The guests, dressed to the nines in elegant gowns and sharp suits, swayed and twirled to the music that floated through the air. The hospital fundraiser had drawn a diverse crowd, from wealthy philanthropists to local business owners, all united in their desire to support a worthy cause.

As the evening wore on and little white lights twinkled overhead, the pastries continued to disappear at an astonishing rate. Lucy found herself fielding a steady stream of compliments and inquiries. Guest after guest approached her, asking for her business card and expressing their interest in hiring her for future events.

One woman, the owner of a chain of popular campsites along the coast, was particularly enthusiastic. "These pastries are simply unbelievable," she gushed, her eyes widening with delight as she sampled a miniature fruit tart. "I'm planning a big Labor Day event at one of my properties, and I would love to have you cater the desserts. Your creations would be the perfect finishing touch to an already spectacular weekend."

Lucy felt her heart skip a beat at the prospect of such a high-profile gig. She had recently invested in a new catering van, and the thought of being able to pay it off sooner rather than later was a tantalizing one.

"I'd be honored," she said, her voice trembling slightly with excitement. "Please, take my card and give me a call sometime next week. I'd love to discuss the details and come up with a menu that perfectly suits your needs."

The woman took the card with a warm, friendly smile.

"I'm Olivia, by the way," the woman said, her eyes bright. "I have a feeling that this is the start of a wonderful partnership. Your talent is truly exceptional, Lucy. I can't wait to see what you come up with for our event."

Lucy felt a rush of excitement wash over her, and she had to fight back the urge to jump up and down with joy.

"Thank you so much," she said, her voice barely above a whisper. "You have no idea how much this means to me. You'll be very happy with the desserts."

As Lucy basked in the glow of her success, Shelby was listening to a conversation between a group of guests who were discussing Penny's poisoning. The topic was still fresh on everyone's minds, and speculation was rampant as to how such a thing could have happened.

"I just don't understand how someone could get their hands on anthrax spores," said a well-dressed man with a neatly trimmed beard. "That stuff is highly controlled. It's not like you can just walk into a store and buy it off the shelf."

Shelby recognized the man as Justin Wyatt, a local pharmacist who owned a chain of drugstores along the coast. She had met him briefly once or twice before when he'd come into the bookshop and had been impressed by his keen intellect and sharp business acumen.

"You're right," a woman said, nodding in agreement. "Anthrax is a highly regulated substance, and it's not something that the average person would have access to. That doesn't mean it's impossible for someone to get their hands on it though, especially if they have connections in the right places."

Justin's eyes narrowed with interest. "Do you have any theories about what might have happened? I can't even imagine how difficult this must be for people close to the woman."

The woman hesitated for a moment, weighing her words carefully. "Honestly, Justin, I'm not sure what to think," she said, her voice thoughtful. "Part of me wants to believe that it was just a terrible accident, that maybe the spores were lying dormant in that old drum, and Penny just happened to be in the wrong place at the wrong time. But another part of me thinks there's more to the story, that someone out there deliberately targeted Penny for some reason."

Justin nodded slowly, his expression grave. "I can understand that," he said, his voice filled with sympathy. "It's hard to imagine anyone wanting to poison someone, but in my line of work, I've seen some pretty dark things, and I know that there are people out there who are capable of just about anything."

Another guest, an older woman with a kind face and a gentle demeanor, spoke up then. "You know, I can't help but wonder if this whole thing might have been some kind of terrible accident," she said, her brow furrowed with concern. "I mean, what if the drum that Penny was using was old and rarely used? What if the spores had been there for years, just waiting for someone to come along and disturb them?"

Shelby felt a chill run down her spine at the thought. It was a possibility that she'd barely considered, and one that made a certain kind of sense. After all, anthrax spores could lie dormant for decades, just waiting for the right conditions to come along and trigger their growth.

"That's a good point, Mrs. Abernathy," Justin said. "It's certainly a possibility that can't be ruled out. Even if that is what happened, it still doesn't explain how the spores got there in the first place. Someone could have introduced them to the drum at some point, whether intentionally or accidentally, or the drum heads were already contaminated. This is sometimes the case with drums imported from Africa."

Mrs. Abernathy sighed, her shoulders slumping slightly. "I suppose you're right, Justin. It's just such a tragedy, no matter how you look at it. That poor girl, fighting for her life in the hospital ... it breaks my heart to think about what she must be going through."

Shelby felt a lump rise in her throat at the words, and she had to blink back the tears that threatened to spill down her cheeks.

"I know her a little from meeting her at my grandson's school," a man said. "Penny is very kind and is an excellent teacher. I just hope and pray that she'll be able to pull through this and come out the other side even stronger than before."

As the conversation continued to swirl around her, Shelby became lost in thought. Even as she mulled over different ideas, she was fairly sure there was more to the story than met the eye. Penny's poisoning had been too targeted, too specific, to be the result of a simple accident.

As the night wore on and the guests began to drift away, Shelby and Lucy walked around the gardens for a few minutes surrounded by the twinkling lights and the gentle rustling of the breeze through the trees. They were exhausted, their feet aching and their backs sore, but the two friends were also filled with a sense of pride and accomplishment that made all the hard work feel worthwhile.

"You did it," Shelby said, pulling her friend into a tight hug. "You knocked it out of the park tonight. Those guests were absolutely blown away by your pastries, and I have no doubt you're going to be fielding calls left and right in the coming weeks."

Lucy beamed at the praise, her eyes shining. "I couldn't have done it without you," she said, her voice thick with emotion. "You've always been there for me every step of the way, keeping me calm and focused when I start to get nervous. I don't know what I would do without you."

Shelby felt a lump rise in her throat at the words, and she hugged Lucy even tighter, letting the warmth of their friendship wash over her like a soothing balm.

"That's what friends are for," she said softly, her voice barely above a whisper. "I know that you're going to do amazing things with your talent and your passion. I'm just lucky to be along for the ride."

As they made their way back to the pastry tent, arm in arm and chatting softly, Shelby felt a sense of unease creeping up her spine. The conversation she'd overheard about Penny's poisoning had stirred up worries and concerns, but she pushed those thoughts aside and focused on the moment, on Lucy's joy and triumph of the evening.

As they stepped into the warmth and light of the mansion's tents, Shelby took one last look at the gardens, at the twinkling lights, and the gentle sway of the leaves in the breeze. It was a moment of pure magic, a glimpse of beauty and elegance.

With that thought in her heart, Shelby turned to Lucy and smiled. "I guess it's time to start packing up. I loved the whole evening. It was so much fun. I'm so happy for your success."

Lucy beamed. "I hope you're going to be helping me with a lot of these events."

"As long as you pay me with pastries." Shelby grinned.

9

The hospital corridors were a maze of bland colors and hushed voices as Shelby and Lucy made their way to Penny's room. The sterile scent of disinfectant hung heavily in the air, mingling with the faint aroma of flowers. It was a scent that Shelby had come to associate with sickness and sorrow, and it made her heart ache for her friend.

As they approached Penny's door, Lucy hesitated, her hand hovering over the handle. "I'm not sure I'm ready for this," she whispered, her voice trembling slightly. "Seeing Penny like this, so vulnerable and weak ... it's going to break my heart."

Shelby reached out and touched Lucy's shoulder. "I know. I feel the same way, but we're here to bolster her spirits. She's strong. She'll get better."

With a deep breath, Lucy nodded and pushed open the door.

The sight that greeted them was one Shelby knew she would never forget. Penny lay motionless in the hospital bed, her once rich brown hair now dull and lifeless against the stark white pillowcase. Her skin looked pale and clammy, and her eyes were closed, the dark shadows beneath them a stark contrast to her pallid complexion.

Shelby felt her breath catch in her throat as she approached the bed, her hand reaching out to gently brush a stray lock of hair from Penny's forehead.

"Hey, Penny," she whispered, her voice cracking with emotion. "It's Shelby and Lucy. We're here to see how you're feeling."

For a moment, there was no response, and Shelby felt a surge of panic rise in her chest, but then, slowly, Penny's eyelids fluttered open, and her gaze focused on her friends.

"Shelby... Lucy..." she rasped, her voice soft compared to the beeping of the machines that surrounded her. "You came."

Lucy swallowed a choked sob. "Of course we came, Penny. We wanted to see you."

Penny managed a weak smile, her lips dry and cracked. "Thirsty," she whispered, and Shelby quickly reached for the cup of water on the bedside table, holding the straw to her friend's lips.

As Penny slowly sipped, Shelby felt a wave of helplessness come over her. She wanted nothing more than to take away her friend's pain, to make everything better somehow. But she knew this was a battle Penny would have to fight on her own, with the help of the doctors and nurses who were working hard to save her life.

After a few moments, Penny's eyes drifted shut again, and Shelby and Lucy shared a worried glance. They knew their friend needed rest, but it was hard to leave her side.

Shelby's mind wandered back to the first time she'd met Penny, a bright-eyed young woman with a contagious laugh and an adventurous spirit. They had bonded over their shared love of books, music, art, and hiking, spending hours in Shelby's bookshop discussing their favorite authors and artists.

Penny had confided in Shelby about a bad breakup with an ex, how her family didn't quite understand her wanderlust, and how her hometown had always felt too small. Shelby's heart ached at the thought of Penny's plans being cut short, of the bright future that had once seemed so certain now hanging in the balance. She reached out and took her friend's hand, silently willing her to keep fighting, to hold on to the hope that had brought her to Hamlet in the first place.

As Shelby and Lucy stepped out into the hallway, they nearly collided with Penny's parents, John and Mary Smith. The couple looked exhausted and worried, their faces lined with the strain of the past few days.

"Shelby, Lucy," Mary said, her voice trembling with emotion. "Thank you for coming. Penny is lucky to have friends like you."

Shelby swallowed hard, trying to find the right words. "How is she, Mary? The doctors, what are they saying?"

John sighed, running a hand through his graying hair. "They say it could take months for her to make a full recovery. The anthrax did a lot of damage to her lungs, and she's going to need intensive therapy and rehabilitation."

Lucy let out a soft gasp. "Months? Oh, poor Penny. She must be so frightened."

Mary nodded, tears welling up in her eyes. "She is, but she's also brave. You know, when she first moved to Hamlet, she was unsure of herself and her decision, but she really likes the town and the people."

John wrapped an arm around his wife's shoulders, his own eyes glistening with unshed tears. "Penny always had a wild streak in her, even as a child. She never quite fit in back home, always dreaming of bigger things, of a life beyond the confines of our small town."

Mary smiled sadly, lost in memories. "When she told us she was moving to Hamlet from Colorado, we were worried at first. It seemed so far away from where we live in California, but it made us realize that sometimes, the bravest thing you can do is to follow your heart, even if it leads you down an unfamiliar path."

Shelby felt a lump form in her throat at Mary's words, remembering the countless conversations she and Penny had shared about the power of following your dreams, no matter how daunting they may seem. It was a lesson that Penny seemed to embody.

As they said their goodbyes to John and Mary, promising to visit again soon, Shelby and Lucy made their way out of the hospital and into the cool evening air. The sun was setting over the rooftops of Hamlet, shining a soft light over the streets.

"I don't know about you, but I could use a drink," Lucy said, her voice still thick with emotion. "And maybe some food, too. I don't think I've eaten anything since breakfast."

As they got into the car, Shelby nodded, realizing suddenly that she was famished. "Let's go to the pub on Main Street that serves those great burgers and fries. I like their selection of local beers, too."

Lucy managed a small smile. "I like that place. I haven't been there in a long time. Let's go."

When they arrived back in the center of town, Shelby parked in her driveway, and she and Lucy walked the short distance to the pub.

The place was warm and inviting, with a fireplace in the corner and a cheerful buzz of conversation filling the air. Shelby and Lucy found a small table near the back, settling in with a sigh of relief as a friendly waitress took their order.

As they waited for their food, sipping on cold beers and trying to make sense of the events of the past few days, a familiar face caught Shelby's eye. It was James Peacock, a retired lawyer who now worked part-time at the library and was an author of crime fiction novels, articles, and books on the history of Massachusetts.

A dear friend of Shelby's, he was sitting alone at the bar, nursing a glass of whiskey and looking lost in thought.

"There's Mr. Peacock."

Shelby and Lucy made their way over to him and Shelby touched his shoulder gently to get his attention.

"Mr. Peacock? Hi. Is everything all right?" she asked.

The older man looked up, his eyes widening in surprise. "Shelby, Lucy. I didn't see you here tonight. I'm waiting for Julie. She's running late. We're going to have dinner together." Mr. Peacock's wife had passed away not long ago, and he and Julie Hall, who had lost her husband three years ago, had become friends. She worked at the library part time after being the full-time librarian there for years. She and Mr. Peacock enjoyed meeting for tea or dinner, walking, going to lectures, and visiting museums.

The young women slid onto the stools beside him, and Shelby's eyes narrowed with concern. "You look pensive, Mr. Peacock. Is there something on your mind?"

He sighed, swirling the amber liquid in his glass. "I'm afraid there's been some terrible news. I just got a text from a friend of mine. There's been a murder, right here in Hamlet."

Shelby felt her heart skip a beat, a cold chill

running down her spine. "A murder? Who was the victim?"

Mr. Peacock shook his head sadly. "A young woman, a tourist who was staying at the bed and breakfast. She was found in her room this morning, strangled to death."

Shelby's mind was racing, trying to make sense of this new information. A murder, hot on the heels of Penny's poisoning? Could there be a connection between the two crimes?

She thought back to the shadowy figure she had seen in her visions, the sense of evil that had surrounded them. Could he, or she, be responsible for both the poisoning and the murder? Or were they dealing with two separate criminals, each with their own twisted motives?

Mr. Peacock's voice lowered to a conspiratorial whisper. "You know, this isn't the first time something like this has happened in Hamlet. Back in the 1920s, there was a string of murders that had the whole town on edge. They never caught the killer, but there were rumors ... whispers of a curse that had been placed on the town by a scorned lover."

Shelby felt a shiver run down her spine at Mr. Peacock's words. She had always been fascinated by the secrets and mysteries that seemed to lurk around every corner of the town, but to hear Mr. Peacock speak of curses ... it made her wonder if there was more to this case than met the eye.

She shook herself. The two recent crimes in Hamlet had nothing to do with the murders from so long ago.

After a bit more conversation, Julie came hurrying over to the bar, hugged Mr. Peacock, and greeted Shelby and Lucy. A few minutes later, as the young women made their way back to their table, their minds still reeling from the news, Shelby knew that Travis would have his work cut out for him.

"What is going on around here?" Lucy took a sip from her glass. "A poisoning and now, a murder."

"It's concerning, that's for sure." A cold shiver ran over Shelby's arms.

As she and Lucy ate their meals, they discussed the two cases and if they could be connected somehow, but everything they talked about was only speculation.

After finishing their dinners, they stepped outside into the cooler night air. Darkness had come to Hamlet once again, but Shelby, with her power of intuition, along with her friends, would give it a fight it wasn't expecting.

10

It was late afternoon when Shelby and Lucy set out to investigate the mysterious person who had donated the drums to the community center. The air was still hot and humid, carrying the scent of freshly baked bread from the nearby bakery and the faint aroma of coffee from the corner café.

Shelby's mind was still reeling from the news of the murder, the pieces of the puzzle slowly forming a terrifying picture. She knew the key to unraveling the mystery lay in the details, in the small clues and seemingly insignificant bits of information that could lead them to the criminal.

As they walked, Lucy turned to Shelby, her eyes full of concern. "So, where do we start? How do we find out who this person is and what their connection might be to Penny?"

Shelby thought for a moment, her fingers absently twirling a strand of her long, brown hair. "Well, we know they were seen at the community center when they dropped off the drums. We can talk to the woman who got a good look at them and see if she remembers anything else about them. Lena, our drum leader, told Travis the woman who saw the person works part time at the yarn store. Her name is Cindy Livingston."

Lucy nodded. "That's a good idea. Then maybe we can ask around town and see if anyone else saw the donor or knows anything about the person. Or maybe Travis could ask Cindy to describe the person to a police artist and then we'd have a picture of them."

"Good thinking. Let's go see if Cindy is working today."

They made their way to the yarn store located in a small brick building on a side street off Main. Inside, they found the woman who had been working at the front desk on the day the drums were donated. Cindy Livingston was a friendly middle-aged woman, who greeted them pleasantly.

"Of course, I remember him," Cindy said, her

eyes widening at the memory. "He was about average height with light-colored hair and a slight beard. He was in a hurry. His posture and his movements had a kind of intense manner to them, like he was on a mission or something."

Shelby leaned forward. "Did he say anything about why he was donating the drums or where he got them from?"

Cindy shook her head. "No, he didn't say anything at all. He just dropped the drums in the foyer and left."

"Could you guess the man's age from the way he moved?" Shelby asked.

Cindy thought for a moment. "I'd guess he was between twenty-five and forty-five. I know that's a wide range, but he seemed reasonably fit. His movements were quick and precise."

They thanked Cindy for her help and left the yarn shop, their heads buzzing with questions and ideas. As they walked down the street, Lucy suddenly stopped in her tracks, her eyes widening with realization.

"Shelby, I just recalled something. Doesn't Penny have a tattoo on her wrist? I remember seeing it once when we were at the beach together. It was a bird and a sun, I think, or something like that. It was very small."

Shelby nodded. "You're right. I remember that tattoo. Didn't Penny once mention something about getting it with an old friend, someone she knew before she moved to Hamlet?"

Before Lucy could reply, Shelby's phone vibrated with an incoming text. "It's Fiona. She'd like us to come by her shop when we have a minute. She wants to show us something."

"Let's go see her," Lucy said.

They hurried the few blocks to Fiona's shop and when they entered, the cool air-conditioned air felt good. Fiona looked up from behind the counter, her eyes twinkling.

"Hello to my two favorite young women. You got here so fast. Were you on Main Street when you got my text?" Fiona came out from behind the counter and gave them a hug. Sixty-five-year-old Fiona Medley was a powerful intuit who owned the Crow's Crossing boutique and had helped Shelby understand and improve her paranormal skills after the young woman had fallen off a ladder at Christmastime.

"We were at the top of Main," Shelby told her. "We were at the yarn shop talking to a woman who saw a man drop off some drums at the community center as a donation. We wondered if he might have something to do with the anthrax poisoning."

"Did you find out who he was?" Fiona asked.

"No, but the woman did give us a good description of him."

"Well, I found something interesting, too. I had some time this morning so I decided to take a look at my shop's security tapes from the night Penny was poisoned. I'd forgotten about them and they were about to be taped over."

Fiona's face grew somber, her eyes clouding with concern. "I saw Penny on my video. It was late at night after the drum circle had ended. She was walking down Main Street when she stopped to talk to a man outside my shop. It was someone I didn't recognize."

Lucy's voice held a tone of urgency. "Can you describe the man,? What did he look like?"

Fiona closed her eyes, her jawline set in concentration. "He was on the taller side. He was wearing a baseball hat, but his hair looked to be blond. There was something on his wrist, maybe a tattoo. On second thought, it was probably a watch."

Shelby and Lucy looked at one another, their hearts pounding with excitement.

Fiona's eyes widened as she stood straight. "Do you think he could be the one who poisoned Penny?"

Shelby nodded grimly, her facial muscles tense and determined. "It's a possibility we can't ignore. We need to find out who he is and what his connection is to Penny. When we see Penny again, we can ask her about him."

Fiona showed the security camera footage to Shelby and Lucy. They saw tourists and townspeople walking along the sidewalk when Penny came into view. A man was walking toward her on the sidewalk, and when she saw him, she stopped short. It seemed she was surprised to see him. They talked briefly. Their body language was stiff. Penny shook her head and as she walked away from him, the man reached out for her arm. Penny shook him off and appeared to speak sternly at him.

"I can't really tell if it's Penny's ex who's on the tape with her," Shelby said.

"The black and white footage makes it difficult to see his face clearly," Lucy agreed.

Fiona promised to send the file to Detective Whitely for his inspection.

"This is such helpful information." Shelby hugged the woman. "I'm so glad you thought to look at the video before it got taped over."

"My intuition must have been trying to tell me something." Fiona smiled with a twinkle in her eye.

Shelby and Lucy thanked her again and left the shop.

As they walked back to Shelby's apartment, Lucy turned to her friend, her voice hesitant. "Do you think the man talking to Penny outside Fiona's shop could be Penny's ex-boyfriend, the one she had the falling out with before she moved to Hamlet?"

Shelby shrugged. "From what Penny told me about him, her ex was more of a controlling jerk than a violent criminal, but who knows? He can't be ruled out."

Lucy nodded, her face thoughtful. "Who else could it be? And what could he want with Penny?"

Before Shelby could respond, her phone buzzed with a text from Travis, asking if he could come over to discuss the case. Shelby quickly replied, inviting him to join her and Lucy at her apartment for pizza.

An hour later, the three of them were gathered around Shelby's kitchen table, two large pepperoni pizzas and a stack of case files spread out before them.

Harper sat in an empty chair at the table with them.

Travis looked tired but determined as he passed slices to the two young women.

They told him about Fiona's security tapes showing Penny and a man talking on the sidewalk in front of the Crow's Crossing on the night Penny was likely poisoned.

"That's an amazingly lucky break. I'll look at the video she's going to send me later tonight."

"So, what have you got for us, Travis?" Lucy asked, her eyes scanning the files with a curious eye. "Have you made any headway on the murder of the woman at the bed and breakfast?"

Travis sighed, running a hand through his short, dark hair. "Not much, I'm afraid. The victim's name is Jennifer Miller, age thirty, from Colorado. She was found strangled in her room at the bed and breakfast. There were no signs of forced entry or struggle."

Harper growled low in her throat. "Ask him if there's a connection to Penny," she told Shelby.

Shelby frowned, her eyes clouded. "Is there a connection to Penny? They both lived in Colorado. Why would someone target both of them?"

Travis's gaze was intense. "That's the thing. I talked to Penny's parents, and they told me that

Penny and Jennifer used to be friends. Apparently, they had a falling out months ago. I'd bet Jennifer was coming here to see Penny."

"This is an interesting twist," Harper said to Shelby's mind. "It could be an important detail."

Shelby felt a chill run down her spine. "So, you think the killer might be someone from their past?" she asked Travis. "Someone with a grudge against both of them?"

Travis nodded, his expression grim. "It's a possibility. I've been going through their old text messages and emails, trying to find any clues or leads, but so far, nothing's jumped out at me except that their falling out was pretty bad. Penny didn't want to speak to Jennifer ever again."

Shelby's mind was racing, her intuition telling her that there was more to the story than met the eye. She thought back to the man who had been seen talking to Penny outside Fiona's shop on the night she was poisoned.

Lucy looked at Travis. "There's something else you should know. Shelby and I talked to the woman who saw the man who donated the drums to the community center. She gave us a good description of him."

Travis's eyes widened, his interest piqued. "I'll talk to her again."

Shelby chimed in. "Penny had a tattoo on her wrist, one that she supposedly got with an old friend before she moved to Hamlet. Did Jennifer have a tattoo?"

"She did." Travis nodded. "On her wrist ... a bird and a sun."

"That matches Penny's tattoo," Shelby told him.

Travis tipped back in his chair, his mind whirling from this new information. "A lot of good details. The man outside Fiona's shop could be key to solving both the poisoning and the murder."

Shelby nodded, her eyes blazing. "It's a strong lead. We need to find out who he is and what his connection is to Penny and Jennifer."

Travis agreed. "I'll put out an alert on the man's description. In the meantime, I'd like you two to keep digging into Penny and Jennifer's pasts. Check out their social media. See if you can find any old photos or messages that might give us a clue as to who this man might be."

Shelby and Lucy both nodded.

"We can do that," Shelby assured him.

"I'll see if I can talk to Penny about the man, or at least ask her parents if they know who he is from the description," Travis said. "And maybe we can get an artist to talk to Cindy Livingston and do a sketch of the man who donated the drums."

"Things are coming together." Lucy smiled and looked at Shelby. "By the way, do you have any ice cream?"

"Yeah, I have a carton of vanilla."

"Great. Let's make ice cream sundaes." Lucy got up and took out the ice cream, some chocolate syrup, and a can of whipped cream from the refrigerator.

Harper trilled her approval and jumped on the counter to supervise.

Lucy reached for some glass bowls in the cabinet. "Come on. Let's have dessert. There's more to life than chasing after criminals. We need some downtime if we're going to be effective."

Travis grinned at Shelby. "She's not wrong."

Shelby chuckled and rolled her eyes. "She rarely is."

11

The day was sunny and hot when Shelby and Travis pulled up in front of the middle school where Penny had been working part-time tutoring students in the summer program. The building seemed quiet and still, the only sound the gentle rustling of leaves in the early morning breeze.

As they walked up the front steps and into the cool, air-conditioned lobby, Shelby felt a sense of unease prickle her skin. The school was usually a place of laughter and learning, of young minds soaking up knowledge like sponges, but today, the halls felt heavy with a sense of foreboding, as if something was amiss.

Travis led the way to the main office, where they were greeted by a stern-looking woman with short, gray hair and a no-nonsense expression. She introduced herself as Mrs. Larson, the school secretary, and ushered them into a small conference room off the main hallway.

"Thank you for meeting with us, Mrs. Larson," Travis said, his voice smooth and professional. "We're here to talk to you about one of your new teachers, Penny Smith. As you may know, she was recently the victim of a poisoning attack, and we're trying to piece together what happened."

Mrs. Larson's face softened at the mention of Penny's name, her eyes showing both concern and sadness. "Yes, of course. Penny is such a lovely young woman, so full of life and enthusiasm. We were all devastated to hear what happened to her."

Shelby asked, "Mrs. Larson, can you think of anyone who might have had a grudge against her, or who seemed particularly hostile toward her?"

Mrs. Larson thought for a moment, her brow furrowing in concentration. "Well, there is one person who comes to mind. Linny Masterson, one of our other teachers. She's always been a bit of a difficult personality, but lately, she's seemed particularly resentful of Penny's success with the students. The students really like Penny and have been doing well with her instruction."

Travis's eyebrows shot up, his interest piqued. "Can you tell us more about Linny? What kind of person is she, and why does she have a problem with Penny?"

Mrs. Larson sighed, her shoulders slumping slightly. "Linny is a bit of a loner, always has been. She's been teaching here for years, but she's never really fit in with the rest of the staff. She's always been jealous of anyone who seems to be more popular or successful than she is, and Penny definitely falls into that category."

Shelby nodded her understanding. "Do you think Linny could be capable of something like this; of poisoning Penny out of jealousy or resentment?"

Mrs. Larson hesitated, her eyes darting nervously around the room. "I don't know. I mean, Linny has always been a bit odd, but I can't imagine her actually hurting someone. But then again, I never would have thought anyone would do something like this to Penny either."

Travis stood up. "Thank you for your time, Mrs. Larson. We'd definitely like to talk with Linny. Would there be time today to speak with her?"

Mrs. Larson pulled up the teacher's schedule on her computer. "Yes, she'll be free in about thirty minutes. I'll send her a notification that someone would like to talk with her during that time. If you'd like to wait in the lobby waiting area, I'll have someone escort you to Linny's classroom in thirty minutes."

"Thank you so much. If you think of anything else that might be relevant, please don't hesitate to contact us." Travis and Shelby moved to the waiting area.

"Linny Masterson. That's a name we haven't come across before," Shelby said. "It will be interesting to hear what she has to say."

Travis's expression was pensive. "It's impossible to know if speaking with her will be helpful, but it's definitely a lead worth following up on. Let's see what we can find out about her and her relationship with Penny."

While they were waiting, Travis used his tablet to dig into Linny Masterson's background, combing through her employment records and social media profiles for any clues or red flags. What he found was a picture of a woman who was deeply unhappy and resentful, with a history of conflicts with coworkers and a tendency to lash out at anyone she perceived as a threat.

But as he dug deeper, he also began to realize that Linny, while certainly a difficult and unpleasant person, was unlikely to be the mastermind behind Penny's poisoning. She had no real motive beyond a general sense of jealousy and resentment, and no clear opportunity to have carried out the attack.

When the thirty minutes had passed, a student escort led Travis and Shelby to Linny's classroom. The woman was hunched over a stack of papers with a red pen in hand. She was a stocky woman with short, blonde hair and what seemed like a perpetual scowl on her face. She looked up at them with a mixture of annoyance and suspicion as they entered the room.

"Linny Masterson?" Travis asked, his voice calm and professional. "I'm Detective Travis Whitely, and this is Shelby Price. We're here to ask you a few questions about Penny Smith."

At the mention of Penny's name, Linny's scowl deepened, her eyes narrowing with barely concealed hostility. "What about her? I heard she got herself poisoned or something. Probably just looking for attention, if you ask me."

Shelby felt a flush of anger rise in her cheeks at Linny's callous words, but she forced herself to remain calm. "Penny is in critical condition, Ms. Masterson. This is a very serious situation, and we're trying to find out who might have wanted to hurt her."

Linny shrugged, her expression bored. "Don't look at me. I barely know the girl, beyond the fact that she's always sucking up to the other teachers and trying to make herself look good."

Travis's eyes focused on the woman. "You did have some conflicts with Penny, didn't you?"

Linny's face flushed with anger, her hands clenching into fists at her sides. "So what if I did? That doesn't mean I tried to kill her or something. I may not like the girl, but I'm not a murderer."

Shelby's intuition was telling her that Linny was telling the truth, that despite her obvious dislike of Penny, she wasn't the one behind the poisoning. But there was still something nagging at the back of her mind, some piece of the puzzle that they were missing.

"Ms. Masterson," she said, her voice soft but insistent. "Is there anything else you can tell us about Penny, anything that might help us understand who might have wanted to hurt her? Were there any conflicts or disagreements she might have had with anyone else at the school?"

For a moment, Linny looked like she was going to refuse to answer, but then something in her expression shifted, and she let out a heavy sigh. "Well, there was one thing. Several weeks ago, I overheard Penny talking to one of the other teachers, Mr. Parrot. He asked her out on a date, but she turned him down. He seemed pretty angry about it, like he wasn't used to being rejected."

Travis's eyebrows shot up. "Mr. Parrot? Can you tell us more about him?"

Linny shrugged, her expression disinterested. "There's not much to tell. He's been here a few years and keeps to himself mostly. He teaches science. He's always had a bit of a reputation as a ladies' man, always flirting with the female teachers and trying to get them to go out with him. I guess Penny just wasn't interested, and she told him straight out that she wasn't in a frame of mind to be dating."

A man who was angry at being rejected and who had a history of inappropriate behavior towards women? He was also a science teacher and might know about anthrax and how to get his hands on it. It was a lead they couldn't ignore.

As they left the school and headed back out into the humid afternoon air, Shelby turned to Travis, her eyes wide. "Elliot Parrot. We need to find out more about him and see if he has any connection to Penny beyond just asking her out on a date."

Travis nodded. "Agreed. I'll start by pulling his employment records and see if there's anything in his background that might raise red flags. I think I should also talk to some of the other teachers to see if they can tell us anything about his behavior or his relationship with Penny."

Travis spent two days following up on the lead, combing through Elliot Parrot's past and interviewing anyone who might have information about his character or his interactions with Penny. What he found was a man with a history of boundary-pushing behavior, who had been reprimanded in the past for making inappropriate comments to female colleagues and students.

But as concerns about Elliot began to mount, Shelby's intuition was telling her that while Elliot could have played a role in the events leading up to Penny's poisoning, he wasn't the mastermind behind it all. She couldn't explain it, but she was sure he wasn't the one who poisoned Penny.

As they sat in Shelby's apartment one evening, studying the case files and trying to piece together the clues, she turned to Travis, her expression filled with frustration.

"We're missing something. I can feel it. There's

something we haven't uncovered yet, some connection that we're not seeing."

Travis sighed, slumping in his chair. "I know what you mean. We've got a lot of pieces, but they're not quite fitting together yet. We need to keep digging and following up on every lead until we find the answers we're looking for."

Shelby nodded, her jaw set with determination. "Agreed, and we need to talk to Penny again, as soon as she's able. She might be able to tell us who she was speaking with outside Fiona's shop on the night of the drumming circle. She might remember some little detail that could help us put it all together." Shelby took a deep breath. "At least, I hope she can."

12

The early morning sun shined through the windows of the hospital room as Shelby and Lucy made their way inside, their footsteps soft against the linoleum floor. The room was quiet, save for the steady beeping of the machines that monitored Penny's vital signs and the gentle rustling of the curtains in the breeze from the partially open window.

Penny lay still and pale against the white sheets, her dark brown hair a stark contrast to her ashen skin. She looked small and fragile, like a delicate bird with broken wings, and Shelby felt her heart clench with a mixture of sorrow and rage at the sight of her friend so helpless and vulnerable.

Lucy moved to the bedside, her hand reaching out to gently take Penny's hand in hers. "Hey, sweetie," she murmured, her voice soft and soothing. "It's Lucy and Shelby. We're here to visit with you, to talk to you for a bit if you're up for it."

For a moment, there was no response, and Shelby feared that Penny might be too deeply asleep or too heavily medicated to hear them, but then, slowly, Penny's eyelids fluttered open, and her gaze focused on her friends, a faint smile tugging at the corners of her mouth.

"Hey, you two," she whispered, her voice hoarse and weak. "Thanks for coming. I know I'm not much company right now, but it means a lot to have you here."

Shelby moved to the other side of the bed, her hand finding Penny's and giving it a gentle squeeze. "We're so glad to see you. You're getting better every day."

For a few moments, they sat in silence, the only sound the gentle hum of the machines and the distant chatter of the nurses in the hallway. Then, Shelby cleared her throat, her expression growing serious.

"Penny, we need to ask you something. Something about the night you were poisoned."

Penny's eyes widened, a flicker of fear crossing

her face. "What is it? Do you know how this happened to me?"

Lucy shook her head, her expression gentle but firm. "Not yet, but we're working on it, and we need your help. Can you tell us anything about the man you were talking to on the sidewalk that night after you left the drum circle?"

Penny's gaze grew distant as she tried to remember. "I ... I don't know. It's all so fuzzy, like a dream that I can't quite hold onto. I remember leaving the circle and heading home. I don't know who I was talking to."

Shelby's heart sank. If Penny couldn't remember the man she had been talking to, they were back to square one, with a few leads and clues to follow.

But then, something caught Shelby's eye. A flash of color on Penny's wrist, peeking out from beneath the hospital bracelet. She leaned closer, staring at the edges of the tattoo, a bird and the sun seemed to dance and shift in the light.

"Penny," she said softly, her voice barely above a whisper. "Where did you get your tattoo? What does it mean?"

For a moment, Penny looked confused, her gaze drifting down to her wrist as if seeing the tattoo for the first time. Then, her eyes widened, a flicker of recognition crossing her face.

"I ... I got it with Jennifer. My friend in Colorado, before I moved to Hamlet. We were very close back then, like sisters. But then ... something happened. Something bad. And we drifted apart."

Lucy said, "Jennifer had the same tattoo as you. What does it mean?"

But before Penny could answer, her eyelids began to droop and her head lolled back against the pillow as exhaustion overtook her.

An expression of disappointment slipped over Shelby's face. "We'll be back to see you soon," she told their friend. "We'll say bye for now so you can rest."

As they stepped out into the hallway, they nearly collided with Penny's parents who were just arriving for their daily visit. They looked tired and drawn, the strain of the past few days etched deep into the lines of their faces.

"Shelby, Lucy," Mary said, her voice trembling with emotion. "Thank you for coming to see Penny. Did you ... did you find out anything new? Anything that might help us understand who did this to our baby girl?"

Shelby hesitated, unsure of how much to reveal,

but then, she saw the desperate hope in Mary's eyes and the pleading look on John's face, and she knew that she couldn't keep things from them.

"We're still piecing it together," she said softly, "but the police wonder if there might be a connection between Penny's poisoning and Jennifer's murder. Did Penny ever talk about the tattoo they got together?"

John's expression was thoughtful. "Jennifer, yes. She and Penny were close friends in Colorado, always having fun together, but then, something happened. Penny never talked about it much, but I got the sense that it was something serious, something that drove a wedge between them."

Mary nodded, her eyes filling with tears. "They had a falling out, a big one. Penny was devastated, but she never told us what it was about. And then, she moved to Hamlet, and we thought ... we thought she was putting it all behind her, starting fresh."

Shelby's mind cycled through the details and clues they'd considered. Tattoos, a falling out between friends, a poisoning and a murder that seemed too coincidental to be unrelated. But what was the connection? What secrets were buried in Penny and Jennifer's past, and who would be willing to kill to keep them hidden?

"Have the doctors given you any updates on Penny's condition?" Shelby asked.

Mary's lower lip quivered as she took her husband's hand.

"It isn't good." John managed to get the words out. "She isn't making the progress they'd hoped. We might lose her."

Shelby's heart sank as she reached out to hug the couple. "Don't give up hope."

"She's a strong young woman." Lucy held their hands for a few moments.

As they said their goodbyes to John and Mary, promising to keep them updated on any new developments in the case, Shelby turned to Lucy, her expression grim.

"I can't believe she might not make it."

"She still might survive." Lucy brushed at a tear that had slipped from her eye. "It's not over yet."

They walked along the corridor in silence until Shelby spoke up.

"We have to stay positive. We'll put our energy into finding out who did this. We need to find out more about Jennifer," she said, her voice low and urgent. "We need to track down anyone who knew her and Penny back in Colorado, anyone who might be able to shed some light on what happened between them."

Lucy nodded, her face looking serious. "Agreed, and we need to take a closer look at that tattoo to see if we can find out what it means and where they got it. There could be a clue there, something that will help us put things together."

As they stepped out into the bright sunlight and heat, the progression of the investigation felt heavy on their shoulders. Shelby sensed they could be on the cusp of something important, something that might change what they knew about Penny and her past.

And so, as they made their way back to her apartment above the bookshop, she felt a quiet certainty that they were on the right track and that the answers they sought were right there waiting for them.

As the sun began to set over the rooftops of the sleepy town, Shelby and Lucy settled in for a long night of research and investigation. Harper sat next to them and watched as they looked over old yearbooks and social media profiles, searching for any connections that might help them unravel the mystery of Penny and Jennifer's relationship.

They sent emails trying to track down anyone

who might have known the two women, and slowly, a picture began to emerge, a story of friendship and loss, and of wounds that never healed.

Through it all, Shelby felt the power of her intuition guiding her, a quiet voice in the back of her mind whispering that they were on the right path and that the truth was waiting for them just around the next bend.

She made eye contact with Harper, and the cat gave a slight nod and swished her tail back and forth.

"The answer is just around the corner," the cat told her.

13

It was another hot, sunny day as Shelby and Lucy made their way down the winding path that led to the rental cabin where Penny's ex-boyfriend, Brent Collins, was staying with his girlfriend. The air was thick with the scent of pine and the distant crash of waves against the rocky shore, a reminder of the beauty that had drawn so many visitors to the sleepy town of Hamlet over the years.

For Shelby and Lucy, there was no time to admire the scenery or bask in the warmth of the summer sun. Their minds were focused on the task at hand, on the questions that needed answers about Penny's past.

As they approached the cottage, a sense of unease settled over Shelby, a prickling at the back of her neck that she couldn't shake off. There was something about Brent that set her on edge, a darkness in his eyes that hinted at an inner anger and resentment that she couldn't quite fathom.

Lucy sensed it, too. "Now I'm wondering if this is such a good idea."

"It's kind of too late now to get cold feet. We'll talk to him, and if he starts to get agitated, we'll leave right away."

They knocked on the door, their hearts pounding as they waited for Brent to answer. When he finally appeared, his face was guarded, his eyes wary and suspicious.

"You're back? Didn't you cover everything you needed the last time you were here with that detective?" he asked, his voice cold and distant.

Shelby took a deep breath, as she tried to find the right words to break through his defenses. "This is Lucy Blake, another consultant to the police department. We were hoping we could ask you a few more questions about Penny and Jennifer Miller."

At the mention of Jennifer's name, Brent's face darkened, a flicker of anger crossing his features before he quickly masked it behind a blank stare. "I don't know what you're talking about," he said, his voice flat and emotionless. "I haven't seen Penny for months, and I barely knew Jennifer. Anyway, that detective was already here asking me about them," Brent told them.

Shelby wasn't buying his comments, her intuition telling her there was more to the story than Brent was letting on. She pressed forward, her voice gentle but insistent.

"Detective Whitely often asks us to do a follow-up interview in case someone recalls something new," Shelby explained. "We know that Penny and Jennifer had a falling out, and we think that might be connected to what happened to them. If you know anything, anything at all that might help us understand, we need to know."

For a moment, Brent hesitated, his jaw clenching as he weighed his options. Then, with a heavy sigh, he stepped back from the door, motioning for them to come inside. "I don't have a lot of time."

Brent led them to a sitting area, his movements stiff and awkward as he perched on the edge of a faded armchair. "What do you want to know?" he asked, his voice resigned and weary, but tinged with annoyance.

Shelby searched his face for any hint of the truth. "The tattoos," she said softly, "the ones that

Penny and Jennifer got together. What do they mean to them?"

Brent's eyes widened, a flicker of surprise crossing his face before he quickly looked away. "They're phoenixes," he said. "They're symbols of transformation, rebirth, and renewal. Penny and Jennifer got them together, back when they were still close. Back before..."

He trailed off, his voice catching in his throat as he struggled to find the words.

Shelby felt a pang of sympathy for him, but there was no time for sentiment. She pressed on, her voice gentle but insistent.

"Brent, we need to know what happened between Penny and Jennifer. We need to know who might have wanted to hurt them, and why."

For a long moment, Brent was silent, his eyes distant and unfocused as he lost himself in memories of the past. Then, with a heavy sigh, he began to speak, his voice low and halting.

"I don't know what happened. Neither one would tell me. They told me it wasn't any of my business."

Shelby felt a surge of anger rise up within her. She knew he was lying, but she forced herself to stay calm, keeping her voice steady as she asked the next question. "And Jennifer's murder? Do you have any idea who might have wanted to hurt her, or why?"

Brent shook his head. "I don't know. I have no idea. Jennifer and I ... we hadn't spoken in months. I had no idea she was even in town until I heard about the murder on the news."

Shelby took a quick look at Lucy, as she tried to make sense of the tangled web of secrets and lies that seemed to surround Penny and Jennifer's past. But before she could ask any more questions, there was a knock at the door and a woman's voice calling from outside.

"Brent? Are you in there? It's me. I'm back from the store. Can you help with the bags?"

Brent's face paled, his eyes darting nervously to the door as he rose to his feet. "You should go," he said, his voice tight with anxiety. "I don't want Sandy to get involved. We're on vacation. I'd appreciate it if you'd leave us alone to enjoy our time together."

Shelby hesitated for a moment, torn between her desire to ask more questions and her sense of empathy for the woman who had unwittingly stumbled into the middle of their investigation. She knew that they had no choice but to leave.

As they stepped outside, they nearly collided

with the slender woman with long blonde hair and piercing blue eyes.

"Oh, hi," she said to Shelby. "You're back?" She looked at the young women with curiosity, her gaze darting back and forth between their faces as she tried to gauge their intentions.

"We just had a few more questions for Brent about Penny Smith and Jennifer Miller," Shelby explained.

Brent walked by carrying three grocery bags and didn't even look at them.

At the mention of Jennifer's name, Sandy's face darkened, a flicker of anger and resentment crossing her features. When Brent was inside, Sandy said, "Jennifer," her voice dripping with venom. "That lying, cheating snake. She got what she deserved if you ask me."

Shelby felt a chill run down her spine at the coldness in Sandy's voice, a sense of unease that only grew as she continued to speak.

"Brent and I have been friends for years," she said, her eyes narrowing as she looked at Shelby and Lucy. "We only got together after Penny left town. Jennifer and Brent had an affair. Jennifer pursued him relentlessly despite the fact he was dating her best friend. Brent was drinking a lot at the time. He was an easy mark. When Penny found out he'd cheated on her with Jennifer, she felt betrayed by both of them. She immediately decided to leave Colorado and found the job in Hamlet. Brent feels very bad about the part he played in the breakup."

Shelby thought back to the way Brent had dodged their questions; the evasiveness in his eyes when they'd asked about Penny, Jennifer, and the tattoos.

Shelby asked Sandy why she and Brent came to the Hamlet area so soon after the breakup. "It seems an odd choice since Brent knew Penny had moved here."

Sandy said, "Brent had wanted to travel to the area for the hiking and the seacoast. He also wanted to see Salem and Boston. We never thought we'd bump into Penny. Brent had nothing to do with what happened to Penny or Jennifer. He's a good man, and he doesn't deserve to be dragged into this mess."

Brent came to the door. "Are you coming in, Sandy?"

Sandy smiled at the man and then turned to Lucy and Shelby. "I have to get going."

As the two friends walked away, a sudden realization hit Shelby like a thunderbolt. She turned to Lucy, her eyes wide with excitement.

"Lucy," she said softly. "What if Brent came to Hamlet for more than just the hiking and the coastline? What if he came here to confront Penny, to try to win her back?"

Lucy's eyes widened, her mouth falling open in surprise as she considered Shelby's words. "You think he might have had something to do with the poisoning?" she asked, her voice trembling with uncertainty.

Shelby shook her head, her mind racing as she tried to fit the pieces together. "I don't know," she admitted, her voice heavy with frustration and doubt.

As they pulled away from the rental cottage and headed for the road that would take them back to town, Shelby said, "I believe Sandy, but I'm not so sure about Brent. He's not telling us the whole story. There's something not right there, something that doesn't add up. We need to find out what it is before anyone else gets hurt."

14

The sun was just beginning to set as Shelby made her way up the winding path that led to Magill's cottage. The air held the scent of wildflowers and herbs, and the gentle hum of bees and birds filled the air.

Shelby's mind was far from peaceful. She knew that Penny's life hung in the balance. The poison that coursed through her veins was slowly sapping her strength and vitality with each passing day.

So, with Harper by her side, she had come to seek the guidance and wisdom of Magill, the most powerful psychic and intuit in New England; the person, along with Fiona, who had helped her understand and develop her own skills. She knew that if anyone could help her find a way to help Penny, it was Magill.

As the young woman and the cat approached the cottage, the door swung open, and Magill stepped out to greet them. The woman had long, silver hair that flowed over her shoulders like a river of moonlight. Her eyes were a deep, piercing blue, and her face was etched with wisdom and knowledge.

"Shelby, my dear," she said, her voice warm and welcoming. "I've been expecting you. Hello, Harper. Come in, come in.

Shelby followed Magill inside, with Harper trailing close behind. The cottage was warm and inviting, with candles aglow and the scent of herbs and spices in the air.

Magill motioned for Shelby to sit, and she sank into a soft, comfortable chair by the hearth. Harper curled up at her feet, her eyes wide and watchful as she took in the familiar surroundings.

"Now," Magill said, her voice gentle but firm, "tell me what troubles you. What brings you to my door on this fine evening?"

Shelby took a deep breath, her heart heavy with the weight of her fears and doubts. "It's Penny," she said softly, her voice trembling with emotion. "As you know, she's been poisoned, and I'm afraid she won't recover. I need your help. I need to find a way to help her."

Magill's face grew serious, her eyes darkening with concern. "I know that Penny has been infected with anthrax," she said softly. "This is grave news indeed, but do not despair. There is always hope even in the darkest of times. I will recite a spell for her."

She rose from her chair and moved to a small table in the corner of the room where a collection of candles and herbs lay scattered across the surface. She began to light the candles, her movements slow and deliberate as she recited a soft, melodic chant under her breath.

Shelby watched in fascination as the candles flickered to life with a soft glow that spread a warm, comforting light across the room. She felt a sense of peace and calm wash over her, a feeling of safety and protection that seemed to emanate from Magill.

"Magill," Shelby said, her voice hesitant. "I'm worried that even with spells, Penny might not have the strength to fight off the poison. Is there anything else we can do to help her?"

Magill paused. "There is one more thing," she said slowly. "I can prepare a special potion that will fortify Penny's immune system, giving her the extra boost she needs to overcome the toxins in her body, but it will require some rare ingredients, and the brewing process is complex."

Shelby's eyes widened, a flicker of hope sparking to life in her chest. "I'll help," she said firmly. "Just tell me what you need, and I'll make sure you have it."

Magill smiled. "I knew you'd say that. Your dedication to your friend is truly admirable. Come, let me show you how to prepare the potion. You can assist me, and in doing so, you will learn a valuable skill that may serve you well in the future."

Together, they set to work, gathering the necessary herbs and oils from the garden and measuring and mixing them with precise care and attention. As they worked, Magill explained each step of the process, her voice soft and patient as she imparted her knowledge to her eager student.

Harper sat nearby and watched Magill closely.

Shelby listened intently, her mind absorbing every detail, every nuance of the complex brewing process. She knew this was more than just a potion, more than just a means to an end. It was a symbol of hope, a representation of the friendship she had with Penny.

When the potion was ready, Magill carefully poured it into a small, glass vial, her hands steady and sure as she placed the cap onto it. She held it out to Shelby, her eyes shining.

"Take this to Penny," she said. "Give her just a teaspoon of the liquid, and it will work its magic, fortifying her natural immune system and hopefully, giving her the strength she needs to fight off the poison. But be careful, my dear. The potion is powerful, and it must be administered with precision. Do not give her any more than a teaspoon."

Shelby nodded, her fingers closing around the vial with a sense of reverence and awe.

"Thank you," she whispered, her voice thick with emotion. "For everything. I don't know what I'd do without you."

Magill reached out and took Shelby's hand, her touch warm and comforting. "You are strong," she said softly. "Trust in yourself and in the power of your intuition, and you will find the way forward."

"I hate to ask for something else, but is there a spell you can say for me that will strengthen my intuitive abilities? I feel muddled and overwhelmed. Penny's life hangs in the balance, and I'm afraid that my intuition alone won't be enough to find the person responsible for poisoning her and killing Jennifer. My focus has been scattered, and I need to concentrate my energies to help Travis solve this case."

Magill reached out and took Shelby's hand in her own, her touch warm and comforting. "Your intuition is a powerful gift," she said, her eyes shining with conviction. "It has guided you this far, and it will continue to guide you in the days to come. I understand your desire for additional support, for a way to strengthen your abilities and focus your mind on the task at hand."

Harper trilled at the woman's words, and Shelby nodded, a flicker of hope sparking in her heart.

"Is there a spell or ritual that can help me? Something that can enhance my intuition and give me the clarity I need to see the truth?"

Magill smiled and nodded. "There is. It is an ancient spell, passed down through generations of wise women and healers. It will not give you all the answers, but it will open your mind and heart to the whispers of the universe, allowing you to see beyond the veil of ordinary perception."

She rose from her chair and moved to a small altar in the corner of the room, where a collection of candles and sacred objects lay waiting. With a wave of her hand, the candles sprang to life, their flickering flames forming shadows on the walls.

"Come, Shelby," Magill said, her voice rich with power and purpose. "Sit before me, and open your heart to the magic that surrounds us."

Shelby rose from her chair and moved to sit cross-legged on the floor before Magill, with Harper coming to sit beside her. The warm light of the candles washed over her, and she felt a sense of peace and calm settle over her mind and body.

Magill began to chant, her voice low and melodic, the words of the ancient language flowing from her lips like a river of molten gold. Shelby closed her eyes and let the sound wash over her, feeling the power of the spell seeping into her bones.

As Magill continued to chant, Shelby felt a tingling sensation begin to spread through her body, starting at the base of her spine and moving upward, until it reached the crown of her head. It was as if a door had been opened in her mind, allowing a flood of new sensations and perceptions to rush in.

Colors became more vivid and sounds more crisp and clear. The scent of the candles and the herbs that hung drying from the rafters filled her nostrils, and she could almost taste the magic in the air.

And then, like a bolt of lightning from a clear sky, a vision flashed before her eyes. She saw Penny, lying pale and still in her hospital bed, the machines that surrounded her beeping and whirring in a constant rhythm. But there was something else, a shadowy figure lurking nearby, a presence that seemed to suck the life from the air.

Shelby's eyes flew open, and she gasped, her heart racing. "Magill," she said, her voice hoarse with fear. "I saw something. A figure, in Penny's hospital room. I think it might be the person responsible for her poisoning."

Harper hissed.

Magill's eyes widened and her voice urgent and intense. "Tell me what you saw ... every detail, no matter how small or insignificant it may seem."

Shelby began to describe what she had seen, the shadowy figure that had lurked in Penny's room, the negative energy that came from the person. As she spoke, Magill listened intently.

When Shelby had finished, Magill sat back in her chair, her eyes distant and thoughtful. "This is a powerful vision," she said, her voice soft. "It is a sign that the spell has worked. Your intuition has been heightened and focused in ways that will aid you in your quest."

Shelby felt a surge of hope. "What should I do now?" she asked, her voice steady. "How do I use this vision to find the person responsible for Penny's poisoning and Jennifer's murder?"

Magill smiled. "You must trust in yourself," she said. "Trust your intuition and the power of the magic that flows through you. The answers you seek are within your grasp, but you must have the courage to reach out and take them."

Shelby nodded as she rose from her seat on the floor. "Thank you," she said, her voice filled with gratitude and respect.

Magill smiled, her eyes bright. "Go now, Shelby," she said, her voice gentle. "Go forth with courage and conviction, and know that the power of magic and love will always be with you, no matter how dark the path may seem."

With those words ringing in her ears, she hugged Magill with the vial clutched tightly in her hand, and then she turned and made her way out of the cottage, with Harper walking beside her.

The hospital was a hive of activity as Shelby and Lucy made their way through the bustling corridors, their footsteps echoing off the polished floors. The air was thick with the scent of antiseptic and the beeping of machines, a constant reminder of the fragility of life and the battles that were being fought within those walls.

For Shelby and Lucy, there was only one battle that mattered: the fight to save Penny's life. They had come armed with the potion that Magill had prepared, a secret weapon in the fight against the poison that coursed through their friend's veins.

As they approached Penny's room, Shelby felt a flutter of nerves in her stomach, a sense of uncertainty that threatened to overwhelm her. She knew what they were about to do was risky and the consequences of being caught could be severe, but she also knew that there was no other choice; every moment counted. She took a deep breath, pushed open the door, and stepped inside.

Penny lay still and silent on the hospital bed, her face pale and drawn and her eyes closed in what seemed a restless, fitful sleep. The machines that surrounded her beeped and whirred, a reminder of the precariousness of her condition.

Shelby and Lucy took deep breaths. They knew they had to act quickly. They couldn't afford to be seen or heard by the hospital staff as they gave Penny the potion.

"I'll keep watch at the door," Lucy whispered, her

voice tight with tension. "You administer the potion, but be quick about it. We don't know how long we have before someone comes to check on her."

Shelby nodded, her fingers tightening around the glass vial in her pocket. She moved to Penny's bedside, her heart pounding as she leaned down and whispered softly in her friend's ear.

"Penny, it's Shelby. I've brought something for you, something that might help you recover from the poison. It's a secret family recipe, and I need you to trust me and take it. Can you do that for me?"

For a moment, there was no response, and Shelby felt a wave of panic wash over her, but then, slowly, Penny's eyes fluttered open, and she nodded weakly, her lips parting.

Shelby felt a rush of relief flood through her. She quickly removed a teaspoon from her pocket and poured the correct amount onto the spoon. She brought it to Penny's lips, tipping the contents carefully into her mouth. She watched as Penny swallowed the potion, her face contorting slightly at the bitter taste.

"What is it?" Penny asked, her voice hoarse and weak. "It tastes strange, but I feel a warmth spreading through me."

Shelby smiled, her eyes shining with relief. "It's a

special potion made by a wise woman who wants to help you. It will give you strength. It will help you fight off the poison that's making you sick. Just rest now, and let it do its work."

As Penny's eyes drifted closed once more, Shelby felt calm settle over her. With a soft smile on her face and a glimmer of hope in her heart, she began to recite the words of the wellness spell that Magill had taught her, her voice low and melodic as it filled the room with a sense of peace and healing.

Lucy watched from the doorway, her eyes wide with wonder as she saw the power of Shelby's magic at work. She knew her friend possessed a gift that was rare and precious in this world.

"That was amazing," she whispered, her voice filled with awe. "I've never seen anything like it. Do you think it will help Penny recover?"

Shelby nodded. "I do. I have faith in Magill's potion ... and in the power of friendship."

With a final glance at Penny's sleeping form and a soft whisper of blessing and protection, they turned and made their way out of the hospital room.

15

It was another hot day as the sun beat down mercilessly on the asphalt of the middle school parking lot where Penny taught, making the air shimmer with heat. Shelby and Travis were a little early for the interview with Elliot Parrot, the science teacher, so they sat in Travis's car with the air conditioning running full blast for a few minutes.

Shelby's thoughts tumbled over one another like leaves caught in a whirlwind. She hoped the meeting with the teacher would prove fruitful and the answers they were looking for were just waiting to be uncovered.

But at the same time, she couldn't ignore the sense of unease that had settled in the pit of her stomach, the nagging doubt that whispered in the back of her mind. What if they were wrong? What if Elliot Parrot wasn't the key to solving Penny's poisoning and Jennifer's murder? What if they were chasing a dead end and wasting precious time while the real culprit slipped further away?

She glanced over at Travis, taking in the determined look on his face and the intensity of his gaze as he scanned the parking lot. She knew he shared her doubts, that he too was grappling with the weight of the responsibility that rested on their shoulders.

"Shall we go in?" Travis asked.

Shelby smiled as she opened the passenger side door. "No time like the present."

They spotted Elliot Parrot heading into the classroom from the hallway, his tall, lanky frame moving with a slightly awkward gait. Travis and Shelby followed him into the room.

"Elliot Parrot?" Travis said, his voice carrying a tone of authority. "I'm Detective Whitely. We have an appointment to talk with you. We'd like to ask you a few questions about Penny Smith."

Elliot turned around, his eyes widening as he took in the sight of the detective and his consultant. For a moment, he looked like he wanted to bolt, his muscles tensing as if in preparation for flight, but then he seemed to deflate, his shoulders slumping and his head hanging low.

"How can I help you?" His throat sounded tight as he gestured to a round table in the corner of the room.

Shelby sat next to Elliot, her expression friendly as she took in the man's obvious nervousness. "We understand that you had expressed some interest in Penny," she said gently. "Can you tell us a little bit about that?"

Elliot's face flushed and his eyes darted from side to side as he struggled to find the right words. "I ... I don't know what you're talking about," he stammered. "I barely know Penny."

But Travis wasn't buying it. His eyes narrowed as he fixed Elliot with a piercing stare. "Come on, Elliot," he said. "We know you asked Penny out several times. We know that you were upset when she turned you down, and we know that you have a history of harassing new female teachers and pestering them for dates."

Elliot's face went pale, his mouth opening and closing like a fish out of water as he struggled to formulate a response. For a long moment, he said nothing, his eyes moving back and forth between Travis and Shelby as if searching for a way out.

Then, at last, he seemed to crumple as he let out a long, shuddering sigh.

"Okay, fine," he said softly. "I did ask Penny out a few times, and yes, I was upset when she turned me down, but that doesn't mean I wished her any harm."

Shelby asked, "Then why did you keep pestering her, Elliot? Why not just accept her answer?"

Elliot's face twisted into a scowl, his eyes flashing with anger and frustration. "Because a person should give someone a chance," he snapped. "It takes time to get to know someone. A man shouldn't be dismissed without having a few dates with a woman to get to know one another first."

Travis's eyebrows shot up, his expression one of annoyance. "Seriously, Elliot? Do you think that women owe you a chance just because you're interested in them? That they should be obligated to go out with you even if they're not interested?"

"How can a woman know if she's interested unless you spend some time together?" Elliot's face flushed an even deeper shade of red, his hands clenching into fists at his sides. "I show interest in some women," he said, his voice rising in pitch and volume. "I'm certainly not pestering them. I don't understand why it's so hard to find a partner these days. I have steady employment and make a good salary. I'm interesting and kind. I like to travel, read, and take walks. Women are too picky these days."

Shelby felt a wave of irritation wash over her, her stomach churning at the thought of the countless women who had been subjected to Elliot's unwanted advances and persistent harassment. She knew all too well the fear and discomfort that came with being on the receiving end of such behavior, the sense of vulnerability that could linger long after the initial encounter had passed.

She also knew she needed to stay focused on the task at hand if they hoped to uncover the truth behind Penny's poisoning and Jennifer's murder so, with a deep breath, she pushed down her own emotions and turned back to Elliot, her manner serious and businesslike.

"Have you ever been in a relationship, Elliot?" she asked.

Elliot's face fell, his eyes growing distant and sad as he seemed to retreat into himself. "Yes, I have," he said quietly, "but they never work out."

Travis fixed Elliot with a stare. "Did you ever wish Penny harm because she rejected you? Did you ever feel like she deserved to be punished for not giving you a chance?"

Elliot's head snapped up, his eyes wide at the suggestion.

"Absolutely not," he said. "I was upset to hear that Penny had been poisoned. I sent flowers to the hospital. I hope she got them. I would never wish ill on anyone, not even someone who wouldn't give me a chance."

Shelby felt a flicker of uncertainty, a nagging sense that there might be more to Elliot's story than he was letting on, but she also knew they had no concrete evidence to tie him to the crimes, and that his behavior, while distasteful, did not necessarily make him a killer.

Shelby attempted to discourage the man's interest in Penny by saying, "Penny is fighting for her life right now. She recently got out of a difficult relationship. Between her illness and her most recent unhappy relationship, I doubt she'll be ready to date for a very long time."

With a sigh and a nod, she turned to Travis. "I think we've heard enough for now," she said. "I think we need to get back to the station. We need to regroup and figure out our next move."

Travis hesitated for a moment, his eyes still fixed on Elliot with a look of suspicion, but then, with a curt nod, he stood up. "Thanks for your time. We appreciate you speaking with us."

Travis's hand rested lightly on Shelby's back as they made their way back to the car, and as they pulled out of the parking lot and onto the main road, a feeling of unease settled over her like a dark cloud.

With a deep breath, she turned to Travis with a serious expression.

"We should talk to Penny's parents again," she said. "We need to find out more about her relationship with Jennifer, about any enemies her friend might have had or anyone who might have wished her harm."

Travis nodded, his eyes fixed on the road as he navigated the winding streets of Hamlet. "Agreed, and we need to take another look at the evidence from the poisoning and the murder. There has to be something we missed, some clue that will lead us to the killer." He turned the wheel to follow the road. "Did you sense anything from Elliot?"

"He really doesn't see that his behavior is inappropriate," she said. "I understand what he says about having a chance to get to know someone, but that can happen by interacting with colleagues on a day-to-day basis. A date is a bit formal and if things don't click between the workmates, it could lead to some very awkward interactions at school."

"That's for sure. I wonder if the school's policy might discourage dating between teachers," Travis said.

"It very well might." She thought about the meeting with Elliot. "My paranormal sense didn't really pick up anything from him. I don't think he poisoned Penny. He did display an angry response to some of our questions, but I just don't see him as someone who would take a life or veer toward violence."

"I got the same impression. I don't see him as the perpetrator."

"Then it's back to the drawing board we go," Shelby muttered.

16

It was early morning in the sleepy town when Shelby made her way down the outside staircase from her apartment and noticed the little door to her mailbox was open. She stopped to shut it but saw a piece of paper inside. She unfolded it and read,

"Meet me at an old hunting cabin in the woods off the Morning Sun Trail today at 7 pm. I have information about Penny's poisoning and Jennifer's murder. Come alone, and tell no one."

A wave of anxiety washed over her. *Someone put this in my mailbox. Who left the note? How did the person know where I live? How did they know I was looking into the cases?*

Thinking about meeting the person, she hesitated, torn between her desire to follow up on the lead and her instinct to proceed with caution. She knew that meeting an anonymous informant alone in a secluded location was very risky, but she also wanted to find out what the person knew. She shook her head. No, it would be foolhardy to go alone.

With a deep breath, Shelby pocketed the note while her mind buzzed over the message and the events of the past week. As she hurried along Main Street to meet Travis at the police station, she could feel tension and uncertainty crackling in the air like static electricity.

She found Detective Whitely in his office, hunched over a stack of case files and reports, deep in concentration. He looked up as she entered, his eyes brightening at the sight of her.

"Shelby," he said with a wide smile, his voice a bit rough from fatigue and stress. "It's nice to see you. What brings you here so early? I thought we were meeting later to go over the latest clues."

Shelby shook her head, her facial expression grave. "I received an anonymous note a few minutes ago ... someone claiming to have information about Penny's poisoning and Jennifer's murder. They want me to meet them at an old cabin in the woods, off the Morning Sun Trail." She placed the note she'd received on his desk.

Travis's eyebrows shot up. "An anonymous note? Where was it left? Did you see anyone leaving it?"

Shelby shook her head again, her frustration evident in the set of her shoulders. "It was in my mailbox. I didn't see anyone. I have a feeling this could be important. We can't afford to let this opportunity slip through our fingers."

Travis reread the note. "You're right, but we can't just go charging off into the woods without a plan. Let me make a few calls and see if I can dig up any information on this cabin and who might be using it. In the meantime, I want you to stay put. We'll go together, and we'll be prepared for whatever we find."

Shelby hesitated, her instinct to take action warring with her trust in Travis's judgment, but in the end, she knew he was right. They couldn't afford to take any unnecessary risks, not when the stakes were so high and the consequences so dire.

"Okay," she said, her voice tight with tension. "I'll wait for your call."

Travis nodded. "I'll work as quickly as I can. In the meantime, try to stay calm and focused. We'll get to the bottom of this."

With those words, he turned back to his desk, his fingers already making the first in a series of phone calls that would set the wheels of the rendezvous in motion.

Shelby left the station, her mind worrying about what they might find at the cabin, and if having Travis there would scare the person off. She tried to push down the fear and uncertainty that threatened to overwhelm her, focusing instead on the hope of finding important information.

Back at the bookshop, the hours ticked by and the sun began to sink lower in the sky, when Shelby's phone finally buzzed with the message she had been waiting for. It was from Detective Whitely, two sentences that set her heart racing and her mind whirling with anticipation.

"Meet me at the trailhead of the Morning Sun trail in one hour. Come prepared for a hike, and bring a flashlight."

Shelby wasted no time, gathering her gear and when it was time to set off for the designated meeting point, her heart pounded with a mixture of fear and worry.

"I should come with you," Harper told her. "I don't like this one bit."

"It's better if you stay here, otherwise I'd worry about you. I'll be with Travis. It'll be okay."

"Be careful, Shelby," the cat warned. "Be aware of your surroundings. Get back home as soon as you can."

Shelby knew an answer might be found at the cabin in the woods, hidden among the trees and the shadows, waiting to be uncovered.

As she arrived at the trailhead, she found Detective Whitely already waiting for her, his eyes scanning the surrounding forest with a wary intensity. He smiled as she approached, his hand resting lightly on the holster of his service weapon.

"Hey, there. Are you ready?" he asked, his manner serious. "We don't know what we're walking into out there, so stay close and keep your eyes and ears open. If anything feels off or suspicious, let me know immediately."

Shelby nodded, her own hand tightening around the handle of her flashlight. "I'm ready. Let's do this."

"My colleagues know where we're going and there's a squad car not far from here," Travis told her. "If I send the signal, they'll be here in seconds."

Shelby let out a long breath, glad to know there was backup for them if they needed it.

Together, they set off into the woods, the trail

winding and twisting before them like a serpent's tail. The air was thick with the scent of pine and the sound of birdsong, but Shelby could feel a sense of unease creeping up her spine, a prickling sensation that told her that something was not quite right.

As they hiked deeper into the forest, the trail began to narrow and the trees began to press in closer, their branches reaching out like grasping fingers. Shelby could feel her heart pounding and her breath coming in short, sharp gasps as the tension and uncertainty mounted with every step.

Just as she was beginning to wonder if they had taken a wrong turn or missed some crucial landmark, they rounded a bend in the trail and saw a small, ramshackle cabin, its windows dark and its door hanging slightly ajar.

Travis held up a hand, signaling for Shelby to stop and stay behind him. He drew his weapon and approached the cabin cautiously, his eyes scanning the surrounding area for any signs of movement or danger.

"Stay here," he whispered.

Holding her breath, Shelby watched as he pushed open the door and stepped inside, his flashlight beam cutting through the gloom and darkness of the interior. For a long, tense moment, there was only silence, broken by the occasional creak of a floorboard or the rustling of leaves in the wind.

Just as Shelby was about to call out and ask if everything was okay, the detective emerged from the cabin, his shoulders slumped with disappointment.

"There's nothing here," he said, his voice heavy with frustration. "No signs of recent activity, no clues or evidence related to Penny's poisoning or Jennifer's murder. It looks like this was just a dead end." He glanced around at the woods. "It could be the person is out of sight, waiting to see if you arrived alone."

Shelby felt her heart sink, the hope and excitement that had carried her this far drained away like water through a sieve. She had been so sure the anonymous tip would lead them to some answers; that the cabin in the woods might hold the key to unlocking the mystery that haunted them.

But now, as she stood there, the only sounds she heard were the rustling of the wind through the trees and the distant call of a lone bird. A sense of despair and helplessness washed over her, threatening to drag her down.

As they were about to turn and make their way back to the car, her shoulders slumped and her heart heavy with disappointment, she heard it.

A sound, faint and distant, but unmistakable in

the stillness of the forest. A sound that sent a chill down her spine and set her heart racing with a sudden, irrational fear.

It was the sound of a footstep cracking a twig as someone walked, slow and deliberate, crunching through the underbrush and drawing closer with every passing second. The sound of the footsteps seemed to be heading straight for the cabin, straight for the spot where she and Detective Whitely now stood, nearly frozen in place.

Shelby's thoughts tumbled over one another in a frantic, chaotic jumble. Who could be out here, off the beaten path? A hunter? A hiker? Why were they heading straight for the cabin?

She took a quick look at Travis, her eyes wide with fear and uncertainty, and she saw the same questions and doubts reflected in his expression. They both knew they could be in danger. Whoever or whatever was approaching the cabin might mean them harm, and they needed to act fast.

17

The darkness of the cabin seemed to press in on Shelby and Travis from all sides, a suffocating presence that threatened to swallow them whole. They huddled together in the far corner of the room. Travis raised his finger to indicate Shelby must be silent. Her heart pounded, drips of cold sweat ran down her back, and her breath came in short, sharp gasps as they strained to hear any sound that might signal the approach of their unknown pursuer.

Travis's hand tightened around the grip of his service revolver, the cold metal a reassuring weight in his palm. He kept the weapon trained on the door, his finger resting lightly on the trigger, ready to fire if necessary.

Shelby crouched beside him, her eyes wide and her face pale in the dim light that filtered through the cracks in the walls. She could feel the fear and tension coiled tight in her muscles, a spring wound to the breaking point and ready to snap at the slightest provocation.

As they huddled in the darkness and waited for whatever fate had in store, Shelby felt they had only succeeded in trapping themselves, in walking willingly into a snare from which it would be difficult to escape.

The minutes ticked by with agonizing slowness, each second stretching out into fear and uncertainty. Shelby's thoughts tumbled over one another in a chaotic jumble of possibilities and scenarios, each one more terrifying than the last.

Who could be out there, stalking them in the woods like prey? What could they want? Could it only be a hiker out in the forest enjoying himself? That's what she hoped ... that whoever it was would walk right past the cabin and go on their way.

She thought of Penny, lying pale and still in her hospital bed, her life hanging in the balance as the poison coursed through her veins. She thought of Jennifer, cut down in the prime of her life, her murder a mystery.

Could the person who'd done those things be the same one who now lurked in the shadows outside the cabin, waiting for the moment to strike?

The thought sent a chill down her spine, a cold, creeping dread that seemed to seep into her bones. She huddled closer to Travis, drawing strength from his solid, reassuring presence.

And then, just as the tension seemed to reach a breaking point and Shelby thought she might scream from the sheer, unbearable weight of uncertainty, it happened.

A quick sound, a creak of hinges and a soft, almost imperceptible footfall, came in from behind them, just yards away. The sound sent a jolt of pure, electric terror coursing through Shelby's veins, a sound that could mean only one thing.

Someone had entered the cabin from the rear.

Travis reacted instantly, his training and instincts taking over as he spun around, his weapon raised and his finger tightening on the trigger. But even as he moved, even as he brought the gun to bear on the shadowy figure that emerged from the darkness, Shelby saw the glint of metal in the intruder's hand, the flash of a blade that seemed to catch the faint light and throw it back in a blinding, dazzling burst.

Then everything happened at once, a blur of

motion and violence that seemed to unfold in slow motion, each moment etched into Shelby's memory with unforgiving clarity.

"Police. Drop your weapon," Travis shouted.

She saw the intruder crouch and lunge forward, a dark, shadowy shape that moved with speed and agility. She saw Travis fire, the muzzle of his gun illuminating the room in a brief, blinding flash, the sound of the shot deafening in the confined space.

At the same instant, Shelby saw the knife; saw it arc through the air, glittering and deadly, and saw it bury itself in Travis's shoulder with a sickening, meaty thud.

Travis cried out in pain, his gun clattering to the floor as he clutched at the wound, his blood already beginning to soak through his shirt and stain his fingers a dark, glistening red.

Shelby screamed, a sound of pure, primal terror that tore from her throat and echoed off the walls of the cabin like the howl of a wounded animal.

She lunged forward, her hands scrabbling for the gun, her mind a whirlwind of panic and desperation. But even as her fingers closed around the grip, even as she brought the weapon up and took aim at the intruder, she felt a blinding, searing pain explode in her arm, a pain that drove the breath from her lungs and sent her crumpling to the floor like a puppet with its strings cut.

Through a haze of shock and confusion, she saw the intruder lift their arm to stab her again, but suddenly Travis moved between them, raising his arm and punching the person in the shoulder.

The attacker stumbled toward the rear door, their movements jerky and uncoordinated as they escaped, vanishing into the woods like a ghost.

Travis fell to his knees. He and Shelby were alone on the ground of the cabin, drops of their blood mingling on the rough, wooden floor.

For a long, endless moment, Shelby lay there, her mind reeling and her arm wracked with pain, unable to move or even think beyond the white-hot pain that consumed her. Then, slowly, through the fog of pain and confusion, she became aware of Travis, of his labored breathing and the soft, pained groans that escaped his lips.

With a massive effort of will, she forced herself to move, to crawl across the floor to where he lay, his face pale and his eyes glassy. She reached out with trembling fingers, her hand finding his, her grip tightening around his fingers as if she could anchor him to her through sheer force of will alone.

"Travis," she whispered, her voice a hoarse,

broken rasp. "We have to get out of here. We have to get help."

For a moment, he didn't respond, his gaze distant and unfocused, his breath coming in shallow, rapid gasps, but then, slowly, his eyes cleared, and he nodded, his jaw clenching with determination as he struggled to sit up, his wounded arm hanging limp and useless at his side. "I'm okay. Are you hurt?"

"He stabbed me in my upper arm. It really hurts, but I'm okay."

Together, leaning on each other for support, they got to their feet, their injuries screaming in protest with every movement and their minds reeling with the trauma of what they'd just endured. They stumbled toward the door, each step painful as they moved their bodies forward and each quick breath a struggle against the weakness that threatened to drag them back down.

Through sheer grit and determination, they made it outside, the fresh air of the forest air hitting them like a slap in the face. The distant sound of birdsong and the rustle of leaves a jarring contrast to the violence and chaos of the cabin.

They leaned against each other, their minds struggling to process what had happened. Shelby's thoughts were a whirlwind of confusion, her mind grappling with the realization that the danger they'd faced was far from over. The person who had attacked them was still out there, still a threat to her, to Travis, and to whoever else they might target.

She turned to Travis, her eyes shining and her voice steady.

"This isn't going to stop us," she said, her hand tightening around his. Her eyes locked on him.

For a moment, his eyes searched her face, then, slowly, he nodded, his jaw clenching with determination. "We'll find out who did this, who's behind Penny's poisoning and Jennifer's murder. We'll get them in the end."

Supporting each other, they made their way back through the woods, back toward the car, and back toward the answers hidden in the shadows.

Finally, they stumbled out of the woods and into the clearing where the car waited. As they climbed inside, their arms and shoulders protesting their movements, Shelby felt a sense of relief wash over her. Their injuries were bloody, but not serious. Stitches would fix them up.

They had survived.

Travis called in the incident before heading to

the hospital so they could be treated. The car sped down the road away from the woods and the attack they'd faced.

If the perpetrator thought he'd stopped them, he was very, very wrong.

18

The sterile scent of disinfectant and the bright, harsh lights of the hospital emergency room were a jarring contrast to the dark, musty cabin where Shelby and Travis had faced their attacker. As they sat on the examination tables, wincing in pain as the doctors and nurses cleaned and stitched their wounds, relief washed over her.

They had survived. The injuries they'd sustained were deep and painful, but they were alive, and that was all that mattered.

As the painkillers began to take effect and the adrenaline of the evening's events started to wear off, exhaustion overwhelmed Shelby and sapped her of the little energy she had left. She glanced over at

Travis, taking in his clenched jaw and the shadows under his eyes, and knew that he felt the same way.

When the doctors finally released them with strict instructions to rest and take it easy for the next couple of days, Shelby and Travis made their way back to her apartment, moving slowly and carefully to avoid aggravating their injuries.

As they stepped through the door, Harper was there to greet them, her eyes wide with concern and her tail twitching anxiously. She rubbed against their legs, meowing plaintively as if to ask where they had been and what had happened to them.

Shelby scooped the cat up in her arms, burying her face in Harper's soft fur as she fought back tears of relief and exhaustion. "I'm so sorry, Harper," she murmured, her voice muffled against the cat's body. "I never meant to worry you."

"I knew you were in trouble," Harper said to Shelby telepathically. "I could sense something terrible happening. I'm never letting you out of my sight. You can't go anywhere without me ever again." Harper purred, her eyes closing as she snuggled closer to Shelby's chest.

As Shelby and Travis settled onto the couch with the cat, their arms and shoulders aching and their minds racing with the events of the evening, they ordered food to be delivered, neither of them having the energy nor the inclination to cook.

While they waited for the food to arrive, they talked softly, their voices low and intense as they tried to make sense of what had happened.

"I'm so sorry, Shelby," Travis said, his eyes filled with guilt and regret. "I never should have let you come with me to that cabin. I put you in danger, and I'll never forgive myself for that."

Shelby shook her head, a determined expression on her face. "No," she said, her voice steady. "I would have gone to that cabin with or without you. I put myself in danger because I knew it was the only way to get closer to answers. You didn't force me to do anything. In fact, I should never have told you about the note in my mailbox. If I'd just gone myself, you wouldn't have been injured."

Travis sighed, his shoulders slumping as he leaned back against the couch cushions. "I still feel responsible," he said softly. "I'm supposed to protect you, keep you safe. I failed at that tonight."

Shelby reached out and took his hand, her fingers intertwining with his as she looked deep into his eyes. "You didn't fail, Travis," she said, her voice filled with conviction. "You saved my life tonight. You fought back, and you got us both out of there alive. That's all that matters."

As they sat there, their hands clasped together, Shelby's mind raced with questions.

"How did the attacker know to contact me? How did he know I was involved in the investigation?"

"Somehow he must have known about your friendship with Penny. He must have seen you with me. He never intended to give you any information. He wanted to get you somewhere alone, either to have you tell law enforcement to back off, to threaten you, or worse. You have to be careful now. Pay attention to your surroundings, stay where there are lots of people, and try not to go anywhere alone."

As the food arrived and they ate sitting on the sofa in the safety and comfort of her home, their bodies and minds exhausted from the night's ordeal, Shelby began to relax, and the coiled tension drained from her muscles.

They finished their meals and curled up together on the couch to watch a movie. With Harper nestled between them like a furry guardian angel, Shelby felt her eyes begin to drift shut, the warmth and comfort of being with Travis and Harper lulling her into a deep, dreamless slumber.

In minutes, all three of them were fast asleep.

When he woke in the middle of the night still on the sofa next to Shelby, Travis wrote her note saying he'd see her the next day and quietly left for his own place.

Hours later, the morning dawned bright and clear with the sun streaming through the windows of Shelby's apartment like a promise of hope and renewal. She called Lucy to tell her about the previous night's ordeal, and within fifteen minutes, Lucy was there to make her a breakfast of eggs and pancakes and to listen as Shelby told her friend everything that had happened.

Lucy held her in a fierce embrace. "That was a very stupid thing to do. You're not a member of law enforcement. Don't ever do something like that again. If you got killed, I'd kill you."

Shelby had to chuckle at her last statement. "I promise I'll be more careful."

"I'm going everywhere with you from now on." Lucy refilled Shelby's coffee mug.

Harper meowed her approval. "See?" the cat said to Shelby's mind. "Lucy thinks like I do."

"I'd like to go see Penny this morning." Shelby ate the last bite of her eggs. "Rachel and Patrice are opening the bookshop this morning. Want to come to the hospital with me?"

"Yes, I do. I have the morning off because I have to work late tonight. Let's go see how Penny is doing."

As she and Lucy made their way to the hospital to check on Penny's condition, a flicker of fear and uncertainty moved through Shelby's mind. They'd been through so much in the past ten days, had faced dangers and challenges she'd never expected, and she was rattled by it.

Stepping into Penny's hospital room with Lucy by her side, Shelby felt her heart drop at the sight of her friend lying pale and still on the bed, but then … a miracle happened.

The doctor entered the room, his face breaking into a wide, relieved smile as he delivered the news they'd been waiting to hear.

"Penny has taken a turn for the better," he said, his voice filled with optimism. "She's still seriously ill, and she has a long road to recovery ahead of her, but we're confident now that she will survive."

Shelby felt tears of relief and gratitude spring to her eyes, her heart swelling with hope. Magill's potion must have worked. Penny was going to live. Reaching out for the young woman's hand, she squeezed it while whispering words of encouragement and support.

"You did it, Penny," she murmured, her voice choked with emotion. "You fought hard, and you won. We're all so proud of you."

Lucy stood on the other side of the bed holding Penny's other hand. "We're so happy. You're going to be all right. We'll be hiking the trails together in no time."

As they left the hospital, their hearts lighter and their spirits lifted by the good news, they headed off to work. Later that evening, Shelby and Lucy would meet at the pub in town to have dinner with Travis. There was still so much to discuss and so many questions that needed to be answered.

Over plates of steaming hot food and mugs of frothy beer, Lucy, Shelby, and Travis toasted to Penny being out of the woods and on her way to recovery.

"We're so happy for her." Lucy sipped from her glass.

"Penny has a long road ahead, but she's going to

make it. She's strong and determined," Shelby said. "And she has a joyful spirit."

Travis nodded and smiled. "This is really wonderful. Thank the heavens." His face then turned serious. "In other news, I had a phone call with Penny's sister, and she confirmed what Sandy said about Brent and Jennifer having an affair. As we know, Penny and Jennifer were close friends back in Colorado," he said, "but then Penny found out that Jennifer had been having an affair with Brent, and everything fell apart."

Shelby felt a wave of anger wash over her thinking about what Penny must have gone through. To have your trust broken by the people you cared for most, to have your heart shattered into a million pieces... it was a pain she could understand, having been cheated on by her last boyfriend.

"The sister also confirmed that Penny broke things off with Brent and cut all ties with Jennifer," Travis continued, his eyes shadowed with sympathy. "She couldn't bear to be around either one of them anymore, so she started looking for a new job. That's how she ended up here in Hamlet."

Lucy asked, "But if Penny wanted nothing to do with Jennifer, why did Jennifer come all the way out here to try and reconcile with her?"

Travis sighed. "That's the million-dollar question," he said, his voice full of frustration. "From what I can tell from Penny's text messages, Jennifer reached out to her a few times, trying to make amends, but Penny wasn't having it. Penny was polite but firm, and she made it clear that she had no interest in rekindling their friendship. She also made it clear she had no interest in seeing Jennifer ever again."

Shelby felt a chill run down her spine at the thought of what might have driven Jennifer to come to Hamlet, despite Penny's clear rejection of her attempts at reconciliation.

"So why did she come here?" she asked. "Who would have wanted to kill her?"

Travis shook his head, his expression troubled. "That's the thing," he said. "Jennifer was strangled in her room at the B&B on the very night she arrived in town. It's like someone was waiting for her; like they knew she was coming and had planned to kill her all along."

Shelby's mind whirled. *Who might have had a motive to murder Jennifer?*

"Could it have been Brent?" Lucy asked, her voice trembling slightly. "Maybe he was angry that

Jennifer had ruined his relationship with Penny, and he wanted revenge."

Travis shrugged. "It's possible. Brent is also a suspect in Penny's poisoning, and we don't have any evidence to tie him to Jennifer's murder. Then there's Elliot Parrot, the guy who was obsessed with Penny, but he probably didn't even know Jennifer. I hate to say it, but Penny would have been a suspect in Jennifer's murder, if she hadn't taken ill that night."

Lucy's eyes widened, her face paling with a sudden realization. "What if Jennifer's death was random?" she asked. "What if the killer just saw an opportunity and took it, without any real motive or connection to Penny, Brent, or anyone else?"

Shelby felt a shiver run down her spine at the thought of a killer who struck without reason or purpose, who took lives simply because they could. It was a terrifying prospect, one that made her feel small and vulnerable in the face of the darkness that lurked in the shadows of Hamlet.

As they finished their meals and paid their bill, Shelby turned to Travis and Lucy, her expression serious and determined.

"You'll figure it out," she told Travis with a steady voice. "And we'll do whatever we can to help you."

"I second that." Lucy smiled.

The three of them stepped out into the night, ready to follow the leads wherever they might take them.

19

Shelby ate her dinner at the small table on the second-floor porch, while Harper sat on the other chair watching the people walking by below them on the sidewalk. It was a lovely warm clear night, and Shelby was enjoying her soup, salad, and hummus sandwich.

Her eyes were distant and thoughtful as she watched the passersby, and her mind endlessly considered the possibilities and theories that had consumed her thoughts for the past two weeks. Ever since Penny's poisoning and Jennifer's murder, she'd been unable to shake the feeling that the answers were just beyond her grasp, hidden in the shadows of the town she loved.

Beside her, Harper sat perched on the edge of

the chair, her eyes fixed on Shelby with a look of concern and understanding.

"We're supposed to be talking about suspects," Harper said to her telepathically.

"I know," Shelby admitted. "I've been deliberately putting it off. I just can't seem to make sense of this case. Every time I think I've got a lead or a suspect, something happens to throw me off track. It's like trying to solve a puzzle with half the pieces missing."

Harper tilted her head, her ears twitching as she considered Shelby's words. "I know it's hard. Shall we discuss it another time then?"

The young woman sighed as a flicker of determination sparked in her eyes. "No. It needs to be done. We have to keep pushing, no matter how difficult it gets. So, let's go over what we know so far."

"Okay." Harper swished her tail. "I haven't been able to be with you when you've spoken to the possible suspects, so my opinions won't be coming from first-hand, or first-paw, experience."

Shelby nodded. "I understand."

"I've listened to you, Lucy's, and Travis's conversations though so I think I have enough background information to ask you clarifying questions." The cat flicked her tail.

"So let's begin. Who do you suspect?"

Shelby sipped her iced tea. "Let's start with Brent. He and Penny were a couple, but she broke up with him after he cheated on her."

"He had a history of being controlling and possessive, and he was in town around the time of the poisoning. Plus, he knew both Penny and Jennifer, which gives him a connection to both crimes." The cat rubbed her whiskers with her paw. "So he might have wanted to hurt Penny for leaving him. He came here for a vacation, which means he could have gone to the community center, made his way to the basement, and poisoned the drum with anthrax."

"How would he know which drum Penny used?" Shelby questioned.

"Aren't there pictures online of her with the drum?" Harper asked. "She always uses the same drum, doesn't she?"

"Yes, to both questions. Anyone who viewed her social media posts would see her with that drum." Shelby went inside to get her laptop and brought it back to the table, where she pulled up the sites that she frequented. "Look." She turned the screen so Harper could see. "There are a few pics of her with the drum." She shook her head. "That answers the question of how someone would know which drum she regularly played."

"So Brent might have poisoned that drum to get at Penny," Harper pointed out. "What about Jennifer? Why would he kill her?"

"He probably found out Jennifer was coming to Hamlet to try to apologize for the affair and ask for Penny's forgiveness. Maybe he went to her room at the B and B to talk to her. Maybe they argued, things got out of hand, and Brent strangled her in a fit of rage." Shelby massaged the back of her neck as she watched a young couple stroll by hand in hand, their laughter carrying on the breeze. For a moment, she allowed herself to imagine a world where love and happiness filled people's lives and where darkness and cruelty were nothing more than distant memories.

"Who else is on the suspect list?" Harper sat up on the chair.

"The man who donated the drums might have wanted to hurt Penny. He could have contaminated the drum heads before he donated them," Shelby explained.

"I don't think that's it. Penny always played the same drum. It's unlikely she would have chosen one of the donated drums." Harper looked at her human companion. "You were at the drum circle the night Penny was poisoned. Did you notice she was playing one of the donated drums?"

Shelby shook her head. "I didn't notice. I never even noticed that Penny played the same drum at each class. I know that sounds strange, but we all sort of get into our own groove when we're playing, and we don't really pay attention to anything except the rhythms we're creating and responding to."

"That makes sense." Harper licked her paw and rubbed the side of her face with it. "The donor of the drums probably didn't have ill intentions. You've mentioned visions of someone entering the community center who you felt had negative energy. Is that person the donor or someone else?"

Shelby's eyes narrowed as she considered the question. "It's not the donor. It's someone else."

Harper stared at Shelby. "You told Magill you saw someone in the corner of Penny's hospital room. The person wasn't really there. The image symbolized the person who poisoned Penny. If you think back, can you see what he looks like, or is he shrouded in darkness?"

"Shrouded in darkness. I can't even tell if it's a man or a woman." Shelby's shoulders slumped.

"This conversation is only making me feel bad. I can't sort anything out. It's all dead ends."

"We're talking things through to make some details stand out and to eliminate people who don't seem to have opportunity or motive. It's a worthwhile exercise. Try to take your emotions out of the equation. Simply look at the facts, and use your intuition. And there aren't only dead ends. Brent remains on the suspect list."

Shelby nodded. "Travis and I interviewed Elliot Parrot, the teacher who persistently asked Penny out. There's something about him that makes me think he couldn't have done such a thing to Penny. He doesn't seem like a violent person. Anyway, what connection could he have with Jennifer?"

Harper's ears perked up, her eyes widening with interest. "Maybe that's something worth looking into," the cat pointed out.

"There's that other teacher at the school, Linny Masterson, who's resentful of Penny for being so good at her job." Shelby brought up the woman she and Travis had spoken to at the school. "But Linny has no connection to Jennifer."

"Have you and Travis completely eliminated the idea that perhaps Jennifer's murder was random?"

Shelby shook her head. "Travis is keeping the

idea open, but I don't really sense that's what happened. I feel Jennifer's death is linked to Penny's poisoning." She paused for a few seconds, thinking. "I'm positive about that at least." In a moment, her eyes darkened and her voice cracked with emotion. "Every day that goes by is another day the killer walks free, another day that Penny and Jennifer's families have to live without closure or justice. I feel like I'm letting them down."

Harper's eyes softened, her purr growing deeper and more soothing as she heard Shelby's distress. "You're not letting anyone down. You're doing everything you can, and more. You've put your whole heart into this investigation."

The young woman managed a weak smile, her hand reaching out to stroke Harper's soft, silky fur. "I just wish I could trust myself, my own instincts and abilities. I feel like I'm stumbling around in the dark, grasping at straws and hoping for a miracle."

Harper nuzzled Shelby's hand, her whiskers tickling her skin. "Your instincts are your greatest strength, even if you don't always recognize it. You have a gift, a connection to the truth that goes beyond logic or reason. You just need to learn to listen to it, to trust in the messages your heart is trying to send you."

Shelby thought over Harper's words. She'd always been a rational, analytical thinker, relying on facts and evidence to guide her actions and decisions. But ever since that fateful day when she had first heard Harper's voice in her mind, she'd begun to question everything she thought she knew about the world and her place in it.

Could it be true? Could her intuition, that quiet, insistent voice that whispered in the back of her mind, be the key to unlocking this mystery?

As she sat there on the porch, the evening breeze caressing her face and the soft, steady presence of Harper by her side, Shelby felt a flicker of something stir within her.

Her eyes widened. "We've met the criminal. I'm sure of it. I don't know who it is yet, but it's someone who's been hiding in plain sight all along. Now, we just need to prove it."

Harper let out a loud trill of approval.

20

It was late at night, but tourists and locals still walked the sidewalks either heading home or going to meet friends at pubs and restaurants. Shelby sat hunched over the counter of her bookshop concentrating on the month's receipts and bills. The shop was closed and quiet except for the sound of rustling papers and the occasional purr from Harper, who lay curled up on a nearby shelf, keeping her human friend company.

Shelby rubbed her eyes feeling exhaustion seeping into her bones like a heavy weight. She'd been working late the past few nights this week, trying to keep on top of the endless paperwork and administrative tasks that came with running a business. But tonight, her shoulder wound ached, and the fatigue seemed to be catching up with her. She could barely keep her eyes open.

With a sigh, she pushed herself away from the counter, gently stretching her arms above her head to work out the kinks in her neck and back. "I think I need some coffee, Harper," she said, her voice rough with weariness. "Want to come keep me company in the back room?"

"Between running the shop and getting involved with trying to solve two crimes, you've been working way too hard." Harper yawned, leaped down from the shelf, and padded after Shelby as she made her way toward the small kitchenette at the back of the shop. As Shelby reached for the coffee pot, she felt a sudden rush of dizziness wash over her, and she had to grip the edge of the counter to keep from falling.

Then, like a curtain being drawn back from a stage, a vision began to unfold before her eyes.

She saw Penny, her face twisted with anger and pain, standing in front of Brent, her fists clenched at her sides. "How could you do this to me?" she cried, her voice breaking with emotion. "How could you cheat on me with my best friend?"

Brent looked away, his face showing both guilt and defensiveness. "I'm sorry, Penny," he said, his voice sounding deep and strained. "I never meant for it to happen, but Jennifer and I ... we just got caught up in the moment, and before we knew it..."

Penny shook her head, tears streaming down her face. "I don't want to hear your excuses. You betrayed me, both of you. I thought I could trust you, but now I see that I was just a fool to think such a thing."

The scene shifted and Shelby saw Jennifer, her eyes red and puffy from crying, standing in front of Penny, her hands clasped in front of her in a gesture of supplication.

"Please," she begged, her voice trembling with emotion. "I'm so sorry for what I did. I never meant to hurt you. Brent and I ... it was a mistake, and I regret it with every fiber of my being."

Penny's face was hard, her eyes cold and unyielding. "A mistake?" she said, her voice dripping with bitterness. "Is that what you call it when you sleep with your best friend's boyfriend? A mistake?"

Jennifer flinched as if she'd been slapped, her eyes filling with fresh tears. "Please," she whispered. "Brent loves you, not me. You're the one he wants to be with. I was just ... I was just a distraction, a moment of weakness, but he never stopped loving you, not for a second. You're the love of his life."

Penny made a harsh, humorless sound that sent chills down Shelby's spine. "If he loved me so much, why did he cheat on me with you?" she asked, her voice filled with a quiet, seething anger. "No, Jennifer. I'm done with both of you. I want you out of my life, forever. Don't call me. Don't text me. Don't even think about me. As far as I'm concerned, you're both dead to me."

The vision shifted once more, and Shelby saw Penny, alone in her room, her face buried in her hands as she wept, her body shaking with the force of her sobs. The pain and betrayal she felt were palpable, a tangible presence in the air that seemed to suffocate Shelby, making it hard for her to breathe.

She watched as Penny picked up a framed photo of herself, Brent, and Jennifer, their smiling faces a cruel mockery of the happiness they'd once shared. With a cry of anguish, Penny hurled the photo against the wall, watching as the glass shattered into a thousand glittering pieces, just like her heart.

Then, as suddenly as it had begun, the vision faded, and Shelby found herself back in the bookshop, her head spinning and her heart racing with the intensity of what she had just seen. She sank down onto a chair, her legs trembling beneath her, and buried her face in her hands, trying to make sense of the jumble of emotions that swirled inside her.

"Harper," she whispered, her voice shaking. "I just had a vision. I saw Penny, Brent, and Jennifer. I saw ... I saw the moment when Penny found out about their affair, and the moment when Jennifer tried to apologize. It was so real, so vivid. I could feel their pain, their anger, and their betrayal. It was like I was right there with them, living through it all."

"Take a few minutes to rest. I know how these visions deplete you." Harper turned her head, and meowed softly, her eyes fixed on something in the corner of the room.

Shelby followed her gaze but saw nothing but shadows and the faint outline of bookshelves. "What is it, Harper?" she asked, her voice barely above a whisper. "What do you see?"

In response to her question, Harper spoke, her voice a soft, gentle purr in Shelby's mind. "Emily is here," she said, her eyes never leaving the corner of the room. "She wants you to know that everything you saw in your vision is true. Penny and Brent, Jennifer and the affair ... it all happened, just like you saw it."

Shelby felt a chill run down her skin at Harper's words, a sense of unease making her head spin.

"Thank you, Emily," she said softly, her voice trembling. "I don't know what any of this means, but I'm grateful for your help."

She rose from the chair on shaky legs. She needed to clear her head to focus her thoughts and sharpen her intuition. There was only one way she knew how to do that.

With Harper by her side, Shelby made her way up the stairs to her apartment, her heart pounding and her head swimming. She knew what she had to do, but she also knew that it would take every ounce of her strength to do it.

As she entered the apartment, Shelby began to prepare for a magic circle. She lit candles, their flickering flames casting dancing shadows on the walls, and turned down the lights, creating an atmosphere of calm and peace. She and Harper sat on the floor, facing each other, their eyes locked in a silent communication of trust and understanding.

"Harper," Shelby said softly, her voice filled with a quiet determination, "I need your help. I need to focus my thoughts, sharpen my intuition, and clear my mind of all distractions. Will you join me in this circle? Will you lend me your strength and your wisdom?"

Harper meowed softly, her eyes shining with

fierce, unwavering loyalty. "Of course, Shelby," she purred, her voice a soothing balm to the young woman's frayed nerves. "I'll always be here for you, no matter what. Together, we can face anything."

Shelby smiled, feeling a rush of gratitude and love for her faithful companion. She reached out and stroked Harper's soft fur, feeling the warmth and comfort of her presence seeping into her body.

Shelby took a deep breath and began to recite the spell she'd learned from Magill, her voice low, steady, and filled with a quiet power that seemed to come from her heart.

"By the light of the moon and the power of the stars," she intoned, her eyes closed in concentration, "I call upon the forces of clarity and intuition to guide me on my path. Let my mind be sharp, my thoughts be clear, and my heart be open to the truth that lies before me."

As she spoke the words, Shelby could feel a tingling sensation wash over her, a sense of energy and power that seemed to flow through her veins like liquid fire. She could feel Harper's presence beside her, a comforting warmth that anchored her to the physical world even as her mind soared.

When the spell was over, Shelby felt a wave of exhaustion wash over her, as if all the strength had been drained from her body. She blew out the candles with a shaky breath, and climbed onto the sofa, her eyes heavy with fatigue.

Harper curled up beside her, a soft, purring presence that soothed Shelby's frayed nerves and calmed her racing thoughts. And as her mind swirled with visions of the past and glimpses of the future, Shelby knew that she had the love and support of her faithful companion.

With a final glance at the remnants of the magic circle and a fleeting thought of Penny and the terrible betrayal she had endured, Shelby let herself be pulled into the waiting arms of sleep, her mind and body surrendering to the healing power of rest and renewal.

21

It was early evening as Shelby and Travis pedaled their bikes along the winding path that ran alongside the river. The air was sweet and warm, filled with the scent of wildflowers and the gentle rustling of leaves in the breeze. Harper sat perched in the basket on the front of Shelby's bike, her eyes wide and alert as she took in the sights and sounds of the woods.

As they rode, Shelby felt a sense of contentment fill her mind. In the beauty and tranquility of nature, it was easy to forget the troubles and worries weighing on her. The mystery of Penny's poisoning and Jennifer's murder seemed far away, distant shadows that couldn't touch the joy and freedom of the moment.

Travis, too, seemed to be enjoying the ride, his face was relaxed and his eyes were sparkling with a carefree light that Shelby hadn't seen in a while. She knew the stress and pressure of the investigation had been taking its toll on him, just as it had on her, but out here, in the warmth of the sun and the gentle breeze, they could both let go of their worries and concerns.

After biking about ten miles, they came to a particularly scenic spot along the riverbank, a place where the water flowed clear and cool over a bed of smooth stones. Shelby pulled over to the side of the path, and Travis followed, both of them eager to take a break and enjoy the beauty of their surroundings.

They climbed off their bikes and made their way down to the water's edge, and Harper leaped gracefully from her basket to follow along behind. Shelby reached into her backpack and pulled out a couple of water bottles and some snacks, handing some of the refreshments to Travis.

"This is exactly what I needed today," she said, taking a sip of the cool, refreshing water. "A chance to get away from it all and just breathe for a little while."

Travis nodded, his eyes fixed on the rippling

surface of the river. "I know what you mean," he said, his voice soft and thoughtful. "Sometimes it feels like the weight of the world is on our shoulders, like we'll never be able to find the answers we're looking for, but out here, in a place like this ... it's easier to refocus and relax." He looked at Shelby. "And having such great company isn't bad either."

Shelby felt a flutter of something warm and tender in her chest at Travis's words, a sense of connection and understanding that went beyond the bounds of their friendship. She knew he was more than just her partner in the investigation, and far more than just a colleague or a friend. He was someone who truly saw her, who understood the depths of her heart and the strength of her spirit.

As they sat there on the riverbank, munching on their snacks and sipping their water, Shelby and Travis made a conscious effort not to talk about the case, not to let the darkness of the mystery intrude on the peace and beauty around them. Instead, they talked about how fast the summer was flying by, the upcoming summer festival in town, and how well Lucy's catering company was doing.

Harper, meanwhile, had wandered off to explore the surrounding area, her natural curiosity and adventurous spirit leading her to climb one of the nearby trees. Shelby watched with a mixture of amusement and admiration as the cat made her way up the trunk with effortless grace, her lithe body moving with a fluid, almost dance-like precision.

"That cat is really something, isn't she?" Travis said, his eyes following Harper's progress with a smile. "I've never seen a cat quite like her before. So fearless, so full of life and energy. So connected to you."

Shelby nodded, feeling a swell of pride and affection for her sweet companion. "She's always been like that," she said. "Ever since she was a kitten, she's had this irrepressible spirit, this need to explore and discover everything she can. I think that's why we get along so well. We both have that same sense of adventure, that same desire to push beyond our comfort zones and see what lies on the other side."

Travis turned to look at Shelby, his eyes shining. "I can see that. You're an amazing woman. Strong, brave, determined. I feel lucky to have you in my life."

Shelby felt a flush of warmth spread through her that made her heart race and her breath catch in her throat. She looked up at him, her eyes locking with his, and saw a reflection of her own feelings, a spark of something that went beyond just friendship.

For a long moment, they sat there in silence, the world around them fading away until there was nothing but the two of them, lost in the magic of the moment.

And then, as if by some unspoken agreement, they both leaned in, their lips meeting in a kiss that was soft and sweet and filled with the promise of something more.

When they finally pulled apart, Shelby felt a rush of joy and excitement, a sense of possibility and hope that made her feel like anything was possible. She looked up at Travis, her eyes shining with light, and saw in his face a reflection of her own happiness.

Travis grinned. "I guess we've decided it's okay to move forward with our relationship."

"I guess so. Is it okay?" Shelby asked him.

"It's more than okay. It feels right." He looked deep into her eyes. "It's strange, but it almost feels like we've kissed before."

Shelby tilted her head to the side for a moment and studied his face. "I know what you mean. It felt so ... familiar."

Travis lifted her hand to his mouth and gently kissed it. "Like it was meant to be."

Shelby's heart melted and her cheeks reddened, then she gave herself a little shake. "Well, we should do this again sometime." Her voice was soft and playful.

Travis chuckled. "Let's go for a hike next weekend and explore some of the trails around here."

She nodded, her smile widening at the thought. "I'd like that. Just the two of us ... and Harper ... out here in nature, and no worrying about criminal cases and mysteries. It sounds perfect."

With a lingering glance and a squeeze of each other's hands, Shelby and Travis climbed back on their bikes while Harper leapt gracefully back into her basket, and set off down the path. The sun was beginning to sink toward the horizon, painting the sky in shades of gold and orange, but for Shelby and Travis, the day was really just beginning, filled with new adventures and the joy of each other's company.

Later that evening, Shelby walked to Lucy's apartment with a bag of takeout food in one hand

and a feeling of warmth and contentment in her heart. Harper padded along beside the young woman, teasing her about kissing Travis.

"Finally. I never thought it would actually happen," the cat said to Shelby's mind.

"Oh hush, you."

"You're both as slow as molasses. It's a miracle you finally kissed."

Shelby had been looking forward to dinner all day, and a chance to catch up with Lucy. She couldn't wait to tell her friend what had happened with Travis.

As soon as Lucy opened the door, Shelby could tell that something was wrong. Her friend's face was pale and drawn, and her eyes were shadowed with a weariness that went beyond mere fatigue. She invited Shelby in with a weak smile, but there was no mistaking the pain and discomfort that lurked beneath the surface.

"What's wrong?" Shelby asked, her voice full of concern as she set the takeout bag down on the kitchen counter. "You look like you're not feeling well."

Lucy sighed, sinking down onto the couch with a groan. "I've been feeling off all day," she admitted, her voice tight with pain. "Just really tired and achy, like I'm coming down with something, but now my head is starting to pound like a drum. I'm afraid it's a migraine coming on, and I don't have any of my pills left."

Shelby frowned, her eyes full of worry. She knew Lucy was prone to migraines, and that when they struck, they could be debilitating. She moved to sit beside her friend on the couch.

"Is there anything I can do to help? Do you have a refill of your pills left?" she asked, her voice gentle and soothing. "Maybe I can run to the pharmacy and pick up the prescription?"

Lucy nodded, her eyes closing against the throbbing pain in her head. "That would be great," she whispered. "I called in for a refill, but I don't think I can handle going out right now. The light and noise would just make it worse."

Shelby gave Lucy's hand a squeeze before standing up. "I'll be back as soon as I can," she promised. "You just rest and try to relax, okay? I'll get the pills and bring them right back. Harper will stay with you."

As Shelby made her way to the pharmacy, she felt badly that Lucy sometimes suffered migraines, but as she stepped through the doors of the brightly lit store, her thoughts were interrupted by a familiar face. Justin Wyatt, the owner of the pharmacy and a man she had seen several times before in her own bookshop, was standing behind the counter.

"It's Shelby, right? I've been to your bookshop," Justin said, his face breaking into a wide, friendly smile. "I saw you and your friend Lucy at the hospital fundraiser a few days ago. Those desserts she made were absolutely amazing."

"Yes, she's really talented."

"I don't usually work the counter, but a few people called out this evening. How can I help you?"

Shelby returned Justin's smile with a slightly strained one of her own. "I'm actually picking up a prescription for Lucy," she said, handing over the slip of paper that Lucy had given her. "She's got a bad migraine and can't make it out of the house."

Justin nodded, his expression sympathetic. "I'm sorry to hear that. Migraines can be really tough to deal with. I hope she feels better soon."

As he checked the bins for the prescription, Justin kept up a steady stream of friendly chatter, asking Shelby about her bookshop and the latest goings-on in Hamlet. She answered his questions as best she could, but there was a nagging sense of unease that she couldn't get rid of, a feeling that there was something off about the way he was acting.

Before she could dwell on the sensation, Justin changed the subject, his expression growing more serious. "I heard about what happened to Penny," he said, sympathetically. "How's she doing? I know you two are friends."

Shelby felt a chill run down her spine at the mention of Penny's name, a sense of unease that made the hairs on the back of her neck stand up. She looked at Justin more closely, trying to read the expression on his face, but his features were carefully neutral, giving nothing away.

"She's still in the hospital." Shelby's voice was tight and controlled. "She's stable now, and the doctors are hopeful that she'll make a full recovery. It's been a tough time for everyone who knows her."

Justin nodded, his eyes filled with what looked like genuine concern. "I can only imagine," he said.

"How do you know Penny?" Shelby questioned.

"I've run into Penny a few times at the community center, and she always struck me as such a kind, caring person. It's hard to believe that someone would want to hurt her like that."

Shelby felt a flicker of suspicion at Justin's words, a sense that there was something he wasn't telling her. She studied his face more closely, trying to read the emotions that lurked beneath the surface, but his expression remained hard to read.

"Do you take classes at the community center?" she asked, her voice carefully neutral. "I don't think I've ever seen you there before."

Justin smiled. "I teach a couple of classes there," he said with a light tone. "I attend a few others when I have the time. It's a great way to stay active and engaged with the community."

Shelby nodded, but the sense of unease that had been building in her gut only intensified with Justin's words. There was something about the way he spoke, something about the carefully measured tone of his voice and the way his eyes darted away from hers, that made her feel like he was hiding something.

But before she could press him further, Justin handed her the prescription and rung up the sale, his smile firmly back in place. "Here you go," he said, his voice warm and friendly once more. "I hope your friend feels better. I'll probably see you in the bookshop soon."

Shelby thanked him and turned to leave, but as she stepped out into the warm night air, she had the feeling that there was more to Justin Wyatt than met the eye. He seemed overly friendly, and there was something about the way he'd answered her questions about Penny and the community center.

As she made her way back to Lucy's apartment, the prescription clutched tightly in her hand, Shelby's body felt anxious and on edge, and she couldn't really pinpoint why.

22

The softness of the lamplight provided a warm, comforting ambiance in Shelby's living room as she settled onto the sofa with Harper curled up beside her. The events of the evening weighed heavily on her mind, and she couldn't shake the unsettling feeling that had crept over her during her interaction with Justin Wyatt at the pharmacy.

Shelby gently stroked Harper's silky fur, finding solace in the cat's peaceful presence. "You know, Harper," she began, her voice barely above a whisper, "something about Justin just didn't feel right. He seemed too friendly, almost like he was trying too hard to make a connection with me. It felt odd, like there was something lurking beneath the surface that I couldn't quite put my finger on."

Harper's ears twitched, and she looked up at Shelby with her wise, emerald eyes, as if encouraging her to continue. Shelby sighed, her brow furrowed in contemplation. "I can't help but wonder if there's more to Justin than meets the eye. Why would he be so interested in Penny? And why did I get such a weird vibe from him?"

As if struck by a sudden inspiration, Shelby's eyes widened, and she sat up a little straighter. "Harper, I think it's time we tapped into my intuitive abilities. Maybe a spell will help me gain some clarity on this whole situation."

With a determined nod, Shelby rose to her feet and began gathering the necessary items for the spell. She placed a few slender, white candles in a circle on the floor, their soft, flickering light making the room feel warm and cozy.

Harper watched intently, her tail swishing back and forth as Shelby settled back down in the center of the circle.

Closing her eyes, Shelby took a deep, centering breath, allowing the gentle energy of the candles to wash over her. She focused her mind, reaching out to the unseen forces that swirled around her, seeking guidance and insight.

"Ancient wisdom, hear my plea,
Let my mind be clear, so I may see.
Allow insight to be my guide,
So I can find the truth that hides."

As the final words of the spell left her lips, Shelby felt a tingling sensation ripple through her body, like a gentle electrical current. Her mind's eye suddenly filled with a vivid image of Elliot Parrot, his face etched with a peculiar intensity that sent a shiver down her spine.

Shelby's eyes snapped open, and she turned to Harper, her voice trembling slightly. "Why did I just picture Elliot's face in my mind? Travis and I don't think he has anything to do with Penny's poisoning or Jennifer's murder. Are we wrong?"

Harper's gaze drifted to the corner of the room, her eyes fixating on a spot where shimmering atoms seemed to dance in the air. The cat's body grew still, as if she were entranced by an unseen presence. Shelby watched in fascination, her heart quickening as she realized what was happening.

"Harper, is it Emily?" she whispered, her voice filled with a mix of anticipation and trepidation.

The cat remained motionless for several more seconds, her eyes locked on the ethereal display.

Then, as if a spell had been broken, Harper blinked and turned to Shelby, her voice echoing softly in the young woman's mind.

"Yes, it was Emily. She told me you aren't wrong."

Shelby felt a chill run through her body. If Emily, the wise and enigmatic spirit, had confirmed her suspicions, then there was no denying the truth. Elliot Parrot was not involved in the dark events that had unfolded.

Leaning back against the couch, Shelby let out a shaky breath, her mind reeling with the implications of this revelation. "We dismissed Elliot as a potential suspect and Emily says we were right to do that. So why do I still feel uncertain?"

As she sat there, the candles flickering softly around her, Shelby knew she couldn't ignore her intuition, that she had to trust in the guidance that Emily and her own inner voice were providing.

Rising to her feet, Shelby began to pace the room, her mind racing.

Harper watched her human companion, her eyes glinting with a knowing look. She understood the turmoil that Shelby was facing, the internal battle between logic and intuition that raged within her. She also knew that the young woman possessed a rare and precious gift, a connection to the unseen world that could not be denied.

As if sensing Shelby's need for comfort, Harper rose from her spot on the rug and padded over to her, rubbing her soft, furry body against Shelby's legs. The young woman looked down, a small smile tugging at the corners of her lips as she bent to scoop the cat into her arms, burying her face in the cat's warm, silky fur.

For a long moment, Shelby simply held Harper close, allowing the cat's soothing presence to calm her racing thoughts, but as she stood there, the candlelight casting a soft, golden glow over the room, Shelby felt a flicker of hope.

With a deep breath and a resolute nod, she blew out the candles and made her way to the kitchen. She would need to gather more evidence to find the missing pieces of the puzzle that would finally bring the truth to light.

As the night wore on and the city slept, Shelby sat at her kitchen table, a steaming mug of tea cradled in her hands and her mind lost in thought … and then Justin Wyatt's face popped into her mind.

The night air was crisp and cool as Shelby and Travis sat at the bistro table on the second-floor porch sipping from cups of tea.

She turned to him, her eyes wide. "Travis, I can't shake this feeling about Justin Wyatt. When I talked to him at the pharmacy, he seemed too friendly, almost like he was trying too hard to make a connection with me. Am I just being paranoid and suspicious about everyone I talk to? Maybe I'm not tapping into my intuition the way I should."

Travis said, "Let's see what we can find out about Justin's classes at the community center. If he's been teaching there, maybe he's seen or heard something that could help us."

Shelby got her laptop and set it on the table, her fingers flying over the keys as she searched for the center's class listings. The soft glow of the screen illuminated her face, casting shadows across her delicate features as she scanned the information before her.

"Here it is," she said, her voice tight with excitement. "Justin Wyatt, teaching "Introduction to Playing in a Band' and 'Basic Italian' this term. So he was telling the truth about that."

Travis's eyes narrowed as he studied the screen. "Okay, so we know he's been at the center. But can you tell me more about what you felt from him? What exactly made you so uneasy?"

Shelby frowned, her brow furrowed in concentration. "It's hard to put into words. It was just there was something lurking beneath the surface that I couldn't quite grasp. I can't explain it, but I know it was real."

Travis sat back and checked his watch. "It's not that late. I think we should pay Justin a visit. I want to ask him if he noticed anything suspicious at the center on the night Penny was poisoned. Maybe he saw something that could give us a lead."

Shelby nodded. "Let me find his address." She returned to her laptop, her fingers once again dancing across the keys. "Got it. Justin Wyatt lives in the next town over. Looks like a pretty posh neighborhood."

Travis raised an eyebrow, a wry smile tugging at the corners of his mouth. "Guess owning a chain of pharmacies pays well. All right, let's go."

As Travis navigated the quiet streets of Hamlet, Shelby hoped the man had seen something on the night Penny had been poisoned.

They pulled up in front of Justin's sprawling Colonial home with its manicured lawns and stately columns.

Travis parked the car across the street, his eyes scanning the property with a practiced gaze. "Looks like someone's home," he said, nodding toward the car parked in the driveway. "Shall we go ring the bell?"

Shelby felt a shiver of anticipation run down her spine. She was about to agree when Travis suddenly stiffened, his hand reaching for the binoculars in the center console. "Hold on a minute. The front door is opening."

He lifted the binoculars to his eyes, his face a mask of concentration as he focused on the figure emerging from the house. For a long moment, he was silent, his body tense with a sense of coiled energy. Then, with a sharp intake of breath, he lowered the binoculars, his eyes wide with shock.

"You're not going to believe who just came out of the house," he said, his voice tight with disbelief.

Shelby's heart skipped a beat, her eyes widening. "Who?" she whispered, almost afraid to hear the answer.

Harper, who had been curled up in the backseat, suddenly leapt onto the dashboard, her ears pricked forward and her eyes fixed on the house with an intensity that made Shelby's skin crawl.

"It's Elliot Parrot," Travis said.

Shelby felt the world tilt on its axis. "Elliot? Are you sure? Why would he be here?"

Travis shook his head, his eyes never leaving the figure now climbing into the car in the driveway. "I don't know, but he's getting ready to leave. Quick, scrunch down so he doesn't see us."

They ducked low in their seats, hearts pounding as they listened to the sound of the car's engine starting up and pulling away from the house. For a long moment, they sat in silence, each lost in their own thoughts.

Finally, Shelby spoke, her voice trembling. "I don't like this, Travis. What should we do?"

Travis took a deep breath, his jaw clenching with determination. "We came here to ask Justin some questions, and that's what we're going to do. Let's go."

They climbed out of the car, their footsteps echoing loudly in the stillness of the night. Shelby's heart raced as they made their way up the driveway, her mind spinning with a thousand questions and doubts.

When they reached the front door, Travis rang the bell, his posture straight and his expression serious. For a long moment, there was no answer, and Shelby felt a flicker of hope that perhaps Justin had left with Elliot and they wouldn't have to face the man who had set her on edge.

But then the door swung open, and Justin Wyatt stood before them, his face a mask of polite confusion. "Hello, Shelby," he said, his eyes darting between her and Travis with a hint of unease. "What brings you here at this hour?"

Travis stepped forward, his badge glinting in the porch light. "I'm Detective Travis Whitely, Mr. Wyatt. I apologize for the late hour, but we have some questions about Penny Smith that can't wait."

Justin's face paled, his eyes widening with a look of genuine concern. "Penny? Has something happened to her? Has she taken a turn for the worse?"

Shelby felt a flicker of doubt at the sincerity in Justin's voice, wondering if the man before them was innocent or guilty.

"Nothing like that. May we come in?" Travis asked, his voice firm but polite. "We won't take up too much of your time."

Justin hesitated for a moment, his eyes darting back into the house as if searching for something, but then he stepped aside, a tight smile on his face as he gestured for them to enter. "Of course, please come in. I'm afraid my wife is out of town at the moment, so it's just me here tonight."

They followed Justin into the foyer, their footsteps echoing off the polished marble floors. The house was even more impressive on the inside, with its soaring ceilings and elegant furnishings, but Shelby couldn't shake the feeling of unease that settled over her like a heavy cloak.

Justin led them into a spacious living room and gestured for them to take a seat on the plush white sofas, settling himself into a high-backed armchair with a look of practiced ease.

"Now, what can I do for you, Detective?" he asked, his voice smooth and confident.

Travis fixed Justin with a piercing gaze. "We understand that you teach classes at the community center, Mr. Wyatt. Is that correct?"

Justin nodded, a hint of pride creeping into his voice. "Yes, I've been offering a variety of courses there for the past couple of years, everything from foreign languages to personal finance. I find it quite rewarding to share my knowledge with others."

Shelby watched Justin's face carefully, searching for any hint of deceit or hidden malice, but the man's expression remained calm and open, his eyes meeting hers with a look of polite interest.

"And is that how you met Penny Smith?" Travis asked, his voice still calm and measured.

Justin nodded again, a flicker of sadness crossing his face. "Yes, that's right. She had recently moved to Hamlet from Colorado and was looking to get involved in the community. We crossed paths a few times at the center, and I found her to be a bright and engaging young woman."

Shelby felt a stab of pain at the mention of Penny, her mind flashing back to the image of her friend lying pale and still in that hospital bed. She swallowed hard, forcing herself to focus on the task at hand.

"Mr. Wyatt, did you notice anything suspicious at the community center on the night that Penny was poisoned?" Travis asked, his voice taking on a bit of an edge.

Justin frowned, his brow furrowing as he tried to recall the events of that fateful evening. "That was about two weeks ago, correct? On the..." He trailed off, looking to Travis for confirmation.

Travis provided the exact date, his eyes never leaving Justin's face.

"Honestly, Detective, I can't say I noticed anything out of the ordinary," Justin said, his voice tinged with regret. "If I'd seen something suspicious,

I would have reported it immediately, but everything seemed normal to me that night."

"What about the day that someone donated those drums to the center?" Travis asked, his voice casual but his eyes sharp and probing. "Were you there when that happened?"

Justin's face lit up with recognition, a small smile tugging at the corners of his mouth. "Ah, yes, I remember that. It was a bit unusual, actually. Someone left a note with the drums saying that they were being donated, but I never saw the donor myself. I helped carry them down to the storage room where we keep all the musical instruments."

Shelby felt a flicker of excitement at this new piece of information. If Justin had been at the center on the day the drums were donated, then perhaps he had seen something, some clue that could lead them closer to solving the case.

But before she could voice her thoughts, Travis was already moving on, his eyes narrowing as he fixed Justin with a piercing stare. "Mr. Wyatt, I couldn't help but notice that Elliot Parrot was leaving your house just as we arrived. Can you tell me about your relationship with him?"

Justin's face went slack with surprise, his eyes widening as he stammered out a response. "Elliot?

He's my brother. Well, half-brother, to be more precise. That's why we have different last names."

Shelby felt a chill run down her spine at the revelation. If Justin and Elliot were brothers, could they be working together, hiding some dark secret that tied them both to Penny's poisoning?

"Did Elliot ever mention to you that he'd asked Penny out on several occasions, but that she'd turned him down each time?" Travis asked.

Justin's face hardened, a flicker of anger sparking in his eyes. "Yes, he did mention that to me. It's a shame, really. I think they would have made a great couple. Elliot is a good man, Detective. He doesn't deserve to be treated like that."

Shelby felt a wave of anger at Justin's words, her skin crawling with the unspoken implication that Penny had somehow been in the wrong for rejecting Elliot's advances. She opened her mouth to speak, to voice her disgust and anger, but Travis cut her off with a sharp look, his eyes warning her to stay silent.

They asked a few more questions, but it was clear that Justin had nothing more to offer them. With a final, curt "thank you," Travis stood to leave, with Shelby following close behind.

As they made their way to the front door, Justin called out to Shelby, his voice smooth. "I'll be sure to stop by the bookshop soon, Shelby. It's always such a pleasure to see you."

Shelby felt a shudder run through her at the man's words, but she forced a tight smile onto her face, nodding politely as she stepped out into the night air.

As they walked back to the car, Shelby could no longer contain the sense of unease that had been building inside her all night.

"There's something wrong about him, Travis. I don't know what it is. Maybe it's only that he comes off as kind of arrogant and entitled. I still don't think Elliot hurt Penny, but what if Justin did? Maybe Justin was angry that Penny wouldn't date his brother."

Travis nodded. "We need to be careful. If Justin is involved in this, then he's not going to give up his secret easily. We need to be smart, to stay one step ahead of him at all times."

23

The sun was shining brightly as Shelby walked through the hospital doors, her heart filled with apprehension. She'd been waiting for this moment, to have the chance to see Penny again and to hear her voice, to know that her friend was truly on the mend.

As she made her way down the sterile hallways, the usual scent of disinfectant and the constant beeping of machines filled the air, always a reminder of Penny's ordeal. Shelby pushed those thoughts aside, focusing instead on the positive, on the fact that Penny was alive and getting stronger every day.

When she reached Penny's room, she took a deep breath, steeling herself for whatever lay beyond the door, but as she stepped inside, she was greeted by a sight that made her heart soar.

Penny was sitting up in bed, her hair tousled and her face still pale, but her eyes were bright and clear, and a smile stretched across her face as she saw Shelby enter.

"Shelby!" she exclaimed, her voice weak but filled with genuine happiness. "I'm so glad you're here."

Shelby rushed to her friend's side, taking her hand in hers. "How are you feeling? You look so good. You're really making progress."

Penny nodded, her smile widening. "I am better. I'm still weak and tired, but I can feel my strength coming back a little bit more each day. And this morning, something amazing happened."

Shelby asked, "What was it?"

Penny's face grew serious, her eyes taking on a faraway look as she reached back into her memories. "I finally remembered who I was talking to outside Fiona's shop, just before I started to feel sick. It was Brent."

Shelby's eyes widened, her heart skipping a beat at the revelation. "It was Brent? Was he following you? Did he threaten you? What did he want?"

Penny sighed, her shoulders slumping slightly. "He wanted me back. He was crying, begging me to give him another chance. I told him no, that I didn't love him anymore and that I never would again."

Shelby felt a surge of admiration for her friend, for the strength and resilience she had shown in the face of such a difficult situation. "How did he treat you? Was he aggressive or threatening in any way?"

Penny shook her head, a small, sad smile playing over her mouth. "No, he wasn't aggressive at all. He was just desperate, I think. He told me he loved me, but I meant what I said to him. I'm done with Brent, with all the pain and heartache he brought into my life. I want a fresh start, a chance to find a healthy relationship that's based on love, respect, and kindness, not on lies and betrayal."

Shelby nodded, her heart swelling with emotion at Penny's words. She knew how hard it was to let go of the past, to move on from a relationship that had once meant everything. She also knew Penny was strong and that she had the courage and the determination to build a new life for herself, one that was filled with joy and purpose.

"I feel free." Penny smiled. "He's in the past. I want to look to the future."

As they sat there, talking and laughing, Shelby could see the toll that the conversation was taking on Penny. Her face was growing paler, and her eyes were growing heavy with exhaustion. Shelby knew that it was time to leave.

"I don't have any stamina yet, but I'm getting better," Penny told her friend. "I think I need to rest now."

"I'm so happy for you. You're doing so well," she said softly, giving Penny's hand one last squeeze. "You need your rest, and I don't want to wear you out. You're beating this thing, and you're going to come out the other side stronger than ever."

Penny smiled, her eyes shining with gratitude. "Thank you, Shelby. For everything."

As Shelby walked out of the hospital and into the bright sunshine, she felt a sense of hope filling her heart. She had to tell Travis what Penny had remembered, and they had to follow up with Brent.

She pulled out her phone and tapped in Travis's number, her fingers trembling slightly with excitement and nerves. When he answered, his voice rough and tired, she couldn't contain the words that spilled out of her.

"It's Shelby. I just spoke with Penny and she remembered who she was talking to outside Fiona's shop that night. It was Brent, her ex-boyfriend. He was begging her to take him back, but she refused."

There was a moment of silence on the other end

of the line, and then Travis's voice came through, sharp and focused. "Brent? She's sure?"

"She seemed positive. She told me what they said to each other."

"We need to talk to him again."

Shelby nodded, even though she knew Travis couldn't see her. "I agree. Are you at the police station? I can pick you up and we can drive out to the cabins together and see if we can catch up with Brent there."

Travis agreed, and Shelby hung up the phone. She knew they were getting close. She also knew they had to be careful. They couldn't afford to make any mistakes or take any unnecessary risks.

She drove through the streets of Hamlet, the sun dappling the pavement with light, and in a few minutes, she pulled up in front of the police station where Travis was already waiting for her. He climbed into the passenger seat, his eyes beaming at Shelby.

"Hey, you." He smiled, leaning in for a quick kiss.

"Hey, to you, too," Shelby said dreamily.

"Let's get this over with," he said, scanning the horizon as if searching for some unseen threat. "We need to talk to Brent and get some answers before he and Sandy leave town and head back to Colorado."

Shelby nodded, her hands gripping the steering wheel tightly as she pulled out onto the road. They drove in silence, each lost in their own thoughts, the only sound the hum of the engine and the distant cry of a lone bird.

When they reached the cabins, Shelby felt a sense of unease move through her veins, a prickling at the back of her neck that set her nerves on edge. She parked the car and climbed out, her eyes scanning the surrounding woods for any sign of movement or danger.

Travis led the way to Brent and Sandy's cabin, his hand resting lightly on the butt of his gun as he climbed the steps and knocked on the door.

There was no answer, and no sound of movement from within.

"Maybe they went on a hike," Travis remarked, his forehead furrowed with frustration. "I should have called first to make sure they were here."

Shelby sighed, her shoulders slumping with disappointment. She had been so sure they would find Brent there and that they would finally get some information that could help solve the mystery of Penny's poisoning. But now, it seemed like they were back to square one with nothing but dead ends and unanswered questions to show for their efforts.

As they drove back to town, the sun sinking low on the horizon and the shadows lengthening across the road, Shelby felt a sense of weariness and despair settling over her. *If only Brent was at the cabin.*

When they reached the police station, Shelby dropped Travis off with a promise to speak the next morning.

As she drove home through the streets of Hamlet, the first stars began to twinkle in the darkening sky. Shelby knew the truth was out there just waiting to be uncovered.

They were close. She could feel it.

The bookshop was closed, but Shelby remained inside surrounded by the comforting scent of books and the soft light of the streetlamps filtering through the windows. She sat at the counter, deep in concentration as she worked through the paperwork and inventory that always seemed to pile up at the end of the day.

Harper lounged on the windowsill, her green eyes lazily tracking the people who strolled along the sidewalks outside. The cat's presence was always a source of comfort for Shelby, a reminder that even in the midst of the chaos and uncertainty that had engulfed her life, there were still moments of tranquility to be found.

As Shelby worked, her mind kept drifting back to the events of the day and the frustrating dead end that she and Travis had encountered at Brent's cabin.

"I wish we could have talked to Brent today." She sighed, glancing over at Harper. "I bet the only reason he planned a vacation to the cabins was so he could see Penny again."

Harper tilted her head, her eyes curious. "You think he's the one who poisoned her?"

Shelby paused, her pen hovering over the page as she considered the question. "It sure seems like it could be him," she said slowly. "But then again..." Her voice trailed off as a sudden thought occurred to her.

"Something doesn't add up. Penny was exposed to the anthrax, but that was before Brent talked to her after she left the community center. If he was hoping to win Penny back, why would he poison her before he spoke with her?"

Harper's ears twitched, her gaze sharpening. "It can't be him then," she said firmly. "It has to be someone else."

Shelby nodded, her mind racing as she tried to

fit the pieces together. "But who is it? Travis and I think the same person poisoned Penny and killed Jennifer," she said. "Brent seems to make the most sense as the perpetrator since he knew both Penny and Jennifer, but it can't be him. Why didn't we see this before?"

Even as the words left her mouth, Shelby felt a sudden wave of anxiety wash over her, a tsunami of fear and a realization that made her eyes grow wide. "It wasn't Brent at all," she whispered, her voice barely audible over the pounding of her heart.

Harper's gaze snapped to the corner of the room where a shimmer of ghostly atoms danced in the air. Emily, the spirit, was trying to communicate with them.

The cat listened intently for a moment, her eyes narrowing in concentration, and then she turned to Shelby, her voice urgent and insistent. "Emily says 'Open your eyes. You know who committed the crimes.'"

Shelby's face went white as a vision of someone's face popped into her head. "Oh, my gosh. I know who it is. I know who poisoned Penny and killed Jennifer."

Before she could say anything else, a loud knock

sounded at the door of the bookshop, startling her and Harper.

Shelby's head whipped around, her heart leaping into her throat as she saw Sandy staring through the window, her face twisted with a desperate, manic intensity.

"Shelby, I need to talk to you," Sandy called out, her voice muffled by the window glass.

Shelby's mind raced, her thoughts tumbling over one another in a chaotic whirl. She looked at Harper, her eyes wide. "Harper," she spoke directly into the cat's mind, her voice trembling with fear. "It's Sandy."

Harper's fur stood on end, her tail lashing back and forth with agitation. "I can see that."

"No, I mean she's the one. She's the perpetrator."

The words hung in the air between them, heavy with the weight of truth. Shelby's heart raced, her breath coming in short, sharp gasps as the realization crashed over her like a tidal wave.

Sandy pounded on the door again. "We need to talk. I need to tell you something."

Shelby's mind whirled, trying to come up with a way out of the situation. She knew she couldn't let Sandy in, couldn't risk the danger that the woman posed, but she also knew she needed to buy herself some time to contact the police and get help.

"We're closed," she called out, her voice trembling with adrenaline. "Can you come back tomorrow? I'm buried with work." The excuse sounded lame even to her own ears, but it was the best she could come up with on the spot.

Sandy's face twisted with anger, her eyes flashing with a dangerous light. She pushed on the door, trying to force the lock, her movements growing more frantic and aggressive with each passing second.

"Please go away, Sandy," Shelby pleaded, her fingers fumbling with her phone as she tried to dial the police. "I can't let you in right now."

Finally, the call connected, and Shelby heard the reassuring voice of the dispatcher on the other end of the line. "I want to report an intruder," she said, her words tumbling out in a rush. "Someone is trying to break into my shop. It's the Spellbound Bookshop. Please hurry."

As she spoke, Shelby's eyes darted around the room. She knew she couldn't stay in the shop; couldn't risk being trapped with Sandy if the woman managed to break through the door.

"Come on, Harper," she said urgently, gesturing for the cat to follow her. "Let's run upstairs."

Together, they bolted for the staircase, their footsteps pounding on the wooden steps as they raced toward the safety of Shelby's apartment above the shop, but even as they ran, Shelby knew they weren't out of danger yet.

As they reached the second-floor landing, Shelby heard a loud crash from below, followed by the sound of shattering glass. Her heart stopped, her blood running cold with fear as she realized that Sandy had broken through the window and was now inside the shop.

She barely had time to process the thought before Sandy burst through the door of the apartment, her face contorted with rage and desperation. In her hand, she held a long, knife, the blade glinting in the soft light of the room.

"Sandy, what are you doing?" Shelby asked, her voice shaking with fear as she backed away from the woman, her hands held up in a gesture of surrender.

Sandy's eyes were wild, her breathing ragged and uneven. "I had to do it, Shelby," she said, her voice trembling with a manic intensity. "I had to stop them. Brent and Penny ... they were going to get back together. I couldn't let that happen."

Shelby's mind raced, her thoughts whirling with disbelief. "What are you talking about? Brent and Penny were never getting back together."

Sandy shook her head, a bitter laugh escaping her lips. "You don't understand. Brent was supposed to love me, not Penny, but he was going to throw it all away to go crawling back to her like a pathetic dog. I couldn't allow that to happen."

A chill ran down Shelby's spine. "You poisoned Penny," she whispered.

Sandy's face twisted into a grotesque smile, her eyes glinting with a mad light. "I had to. I had to stop her from taking Brent away from me. Now, I've taken care of Brent, too. He's dead, Shelby. I killed him at the cabin a few hours ago. He deserved it. I couldn't let him live."

Shelby's mind reeled, her stomach churning with horror and revulsion. She knew she had to keep Sandy talking to find a way to stall for time until help could arrive.

"How did you do it?" she asked, her voice trembling with fear. "How could you get hold of anthrax spores?"

Sandy let out a harsh, barking laugh, her eyes flashing with a twisted pride. "I used to work in a lab where they researched anthrax, among other things.

From working there, I knew there was a dark network where you can get just about anything."

Shelby's thoughts swirled with the need to understand. "How did you get access to the drums?"

Sandy's smile widened, her teeth flashing in the dim light of the room. "It wasn't very hard. I went to the community center to ask about joining the drum circle. I saw Penny on social media playing a drum. She posted where she was and what she was doing, and that she always chose the same drum."

The woman paused, her forehead beading with sweat as she relived the memory.

"I asked the woman at the desk if I could see the kinds of drums I could play. She told me they were stored in the basement, and I'd have to come to the class to try the drums."

Shelby's breath came in short, sharp gasps as she listened to Sandy's confession.

"When no one was looking, I headed to the basement and into the storage room," Sandy continued, her voice rising with intensity. "I planted the spores on the head of the drum Penny always played. I thought everything went well, but Penny didn't get sick enough. My next stop after this will be the hospital to finish what I started."

Shelby's blood ran cold at the thought of Sandy

going after Penny again, of the woman's twisted obsession leading to even more violence and death.

"You killed Jennifer?" she whispered.

Sandy's face contorted with rage and jealousy, her eyes blazing with a fevered light. "I had to get rid of that cheating cow, too. There was no way I was letting Brent crawl back to her or Penny."

With a sudden, violent movement, Sandy brandished the knife, the blade glinting in the dim light of the room. "Call Detective Whitely," she demanded, her voice cold and hard. "Get him to come here. When he arrives, you'll be dead."

Shelby's heart almost stopped, her blood running cold with fear as Sandy stepped forward, the knife held out in front of her like a deadly promise.

"Wait," Shelby stammered, her hands shaking as she backed away from the woman. "I'm no threat to you. I won't tell anyone what you did."

But Sandy only cackled, her laughter harsh and grating in the stillness of the room. "Right, Shelby. Just call the detective."

Shelby's thoughts scrambled for a way out. She couldn't let the woman's twisted obsession claim any more victims.

"If Travis comes here, you'll be sorry," she said,

her voice trembling. "Your best chance is to get out of here and run. It's possible no one will ever find you, but you have to go now."

Sandy only screamed in response, her face contorted with rage and madness. "Call him!"

Shelby shook her head, her resolve hardening even as her heart pounded with terror. "I won't."

Then, in a moment of pure, blind fury, Sandy lunged at Shelby, her knife flashing. Shelby braced herself for the impact, ready to use all of her strength to punch Sandy in the face.

But the moment never came.

Instead, she heard a fierce, animalistic yowl, followed by a scream of pain and surprise. She saw Harper clinging to Sandy's back, her claws digging deep into the woman's flesh.

Shelby seized the moment of distraction, sidestepping Sandy's wild, flailing attack and stumbling back toward the bookshelves. And then, as if by a miracle, a heavy book flew off one of the shelves, hurtling through the air and slamming into Sandy's face with a sickening thud.

The woman swayed for a moment, her eyes rolling back in her head as she teetered on the brink of consciousness. Then, with a final, shuddering gasp, she collapsed, the knife clattering harmlessly onto the floor.

Shelby and Harper stood there, their jaws slack with shock and disbelief as they stared at Sandy's unconscious form. As the realization of what had just happened began to sink in, Harper's eyes widened with sudden understanding.

"Thank you, Emily," the cat told the ghost, then spoke to Shelby's mind. "I didn't know she had such a strong arm."

Before Shelby could respond, the door to the apartment burst open, and Travis and two other officers rushed in, their guns drawn and their faces tense with worry and determination, but when they saw Sandy lying motionless on the floor, their expressions changed to ones of relief.

Travis holstered his weapon and rushed to Shelby's side, wrapping her in a tight, protective hug. "Are you all right?" he asked, his voice rough with emotion.

Shelby nodded, her own arms coming up to hold Travis as she buried her face in his chest.

"I am now," she whispered, her voice muffled by the fabric of his shirt.

24

The setting sun created a dazzling sparkle on the water as the magnificent yacht sailed smoothly through the waves. On board, the atmosphere was one of celebration and joy, as the wealthy couple hosted their fiftieth wedding anniversary party surrounded by family, friends, and the stunning beauty of the sea.

Shelby stood on the deck, her long black gown fluttering gently in the breeze as she took in the scene before her. She had come along to help Lucy, who was catering the event, and the two of them had spent the day working to ensure that everything was perfect.

As she watched the guests mingle and laugh, sipping champagne and sampling the delectable desserts Lucy had prepared, Shelby felt happy. She knew how much this event meant to Lucy, how hard she'd been working to get her catering business started, and seeing her friend's plans come to fruition was a true joy.

Inside the yacht, the salon was a hive of activity with guests moving seamlessly between the buffet table, the dining room, and the aft deck. The quartet of musicians played soft, melodic tunes that drifted through the air, adding to the ambiance of the evening.

Shelby's gaze was drawn to the dessert buffet table, which was a true work of art. Tiered stands overflowed with an array of colorful and tempting sweets, from delicate macarons to rich chocolate truffles. The table was adorned with beautiful floral arrangements and elegant fabric draping, creating a stunning visual display that was as lovely as the taste of the sweets.

Lucy stood behind the table, her navy dress shimmering in the soft light as she greeted guests with a warm smile and offered them their choice of desserts. Shelby joined her, the two of them working in harmony as they served the guests and ensured that the buffet remained fully stocked.

From time to time, Ross and Travis, both looking

dashing in their tuxedos, would appear from the storage area, their arms laden with trays of sweets and fresh pastries to replenish the table. Shelby admired the easy way they moved, their strong and capable hands making light work of the heavy trays.

As the evening wore on and the guests began to drift toward the dance floor, Lucy and Shelby finally had a moment to breathe. They'd been told that once the focus shifted to dancing and drinking, they were free to join in the festivities as long as they kept the dessert buffet well-stocked for self-service.

Getting some drinks from one of the bars, the four friends made their way to one of the yacht's decks, the stars twinkling brightly overhead in the inky black sky. The air was warm and balmy, the gentle breeze carrying with it the scent of the sea and the faint strains of music from inside.

"What an incredible night." Lucy sighed, her eyes shining with joy. "I can't believe how well everything's gone. I've already had inquiries about catering two more events like this one."

Shelby smiled, her heart swelling with joy. "I'm so proud of you. You've worked so hard to get to this point, and it's all paying off. Your business is really taking off, and I couldn't be happier for you."

Ross and Travis nodded in agreement, their faces beaming.

"You're a true talent," Ross told her with warmth and sincerity. "Anyone would be lucky to have you cater their event."

As the four of them stood there, sipping their drinks and savoring the moment, Shelby's mind drifted back to the case they'd just solved.

"We never did figure out who donated the drums to the community center," she noted.

"It doesn't matter now though," Travis said.

"I really need to work on my intuitive skills. I finally figured out it was Sandy, but it was almost too late."

"You've only had these skills for eight months," Travis reminded her. "You're improving all the time."

"It's still hard to believe, isn't it?" Shelby said softly, her gaze fixed on the distant horizon. "Everything that happened with Penny, Jennifer, Brent, and Sandy ... the betrayal, the temptation, the jealousy, the revenge. It's just so sad."

Travis nodded, his face somber as he considered her words. "It is sad. Two people dead, and one poisoned and facing months of recovery. It's a stark reminder of just how far some people will go when they're consumed by their own darkness."

Shelby turned to him, her eyes searching his face. "How do you do it, Travis? How do you hold up in the face of all the awful things you see in your line of work? You see the absolute worst of humanity, day in and day out."

Travis was quiet for a moment, his gaze distant as he considered her question. When he spoke, his voice was low and thoughtful, filled with a quiet strength that Shelby had come to admire.

"It's true, I do see the worst of humanity sometimes. The cruelty, the selfishness, the disregard for human life. It can definitely bring me down, make me question the good in the world."

He paused, his eyes meeting Shelby's with an intensity that made her heart skip a beat. "But I also see the very best of humanity every single day. People who give of themselves to protect, help, and save others. People who step in when they see a wrong or an injustice, who put themselves in danger to do what's right. Every day I see ordinary people who do extraordinary things."

Shelby felt a smile tug at the corners of her mouth, a warmth spreading through her chest at his words. "You know, you just described yourself perfectly."

Travis shook his head, a soft chuckle escaping

his lips. "But it also describes you, Shelby. The way you've fought for the truth, the way you've put yourself on the line to help others and bring justice to those who have been wronged. You're one of the most extraordinary people I know."

Shelby felt a blush rise in her cheeks, her heart swelling with emotion. She stepped closer to him, her arms wrapping around his waist as she rested her head against his chest. She could hear the steady thrum of his heartbeat and feel the warmth of his body seeping into her own.

As they stood there, lost in each other's embrace, Shelby's mind drifted back over the events of the past few weeks; the mystery, the danger, the twists and turns. It had been a journey filled with heartache and fear, with moments of despair and doubt.

But it had also been a journey of learning to trust in herself and in those around her. As she stood there on the deck of the yacht, the stars shining down on them like a thousand tiny sparks, Shelby knew that she was exactly where she was meant to be. She had the feeling she was with a man who would be her anchor, and she hoped she would always be his.

As the yacht sailed on into the night, she knew

her story was still being written, page by page and chapter by chapter, and wondered how on earth she'd gotten so lucky.

I hope you enjoyed *Poison and Potions*! The next book in the series, *Legends and Luck*, can be found here:

https://mybook.to/LegendsandLuck

THANK YOU FOR READING!

Books by J.A. WHITING can be found here:
amazon.com/author/jawhiting

To hear about new books and book sales, please sign up for my mailing list at:
jawhiting.com

Your email will never be sold, shared, or spammed.

If you enjoyed the book, please consider leaving a review. A few words are all that's needed. It would be very much appreciated.

BOOKS BY J. A. WHITING

SPELLBOUND BOOKSHOP PARANORMAL COZY MYSTERIES

SWEET COVE PARANORMAL COZY MYSTERIES

LIN COFFIN PARANORMAL COZY MYSTERIES

CLAIRE ROLLINS PARANORMAL COZY MYSTERIES

MURDER POSSE PARANORMAL COZY MYSTERIES

PAXTON PARK PARANORMAL COZY MYSTERIES

ELLA DANIELS WITCH COZY MYSTERIES

SEEING COLORS PARANORMAL COZY MYSTERIES

OLIVIA MILLER MYSTERIES (not cozy)

SWEET ROMANCES by JENA WINTER

COZY BOX SETS

BOOKS BY J.A. WHITING & NELL MCCARTHY

HOPE HERRING PARANORMAL COZY MYSTERIES

TIPPERARY CARRIAGE COMPANY COZY MYSTERIES

BOOKS BY J.A. WHITING & ARIEL SLICK

GOOD HARBOR WITCHES PARANORMAL COZY MYSTERIES

BOOKS BY J.A. WHITING & AMANDA DIAMOND

PEACHTREE POINT COZY MYSTERIES

DIGGING UP SECRETS PARANORMAL COZY MYSTERIES

BOOKS BY J.A. WHITING & MAY STENMARK

MAGICAL SLEUTH PARANORMAL WOMEN'S FICTION COZY MYSTERIES

HALF MOON PARANORMAL MYSTERIES

VISIT US

jawhiting.com

bookbub.com/authors/j-a-whiting

amazon.com/author/jawhiting

facebook.com/jawhitingauthor

bingebooks.com/author/ja-whiting

Made in United States
North Haven, CT
23 September 2024